LIGHT OF MY LIFE

1840s Cornwall. Meg Deveral and her father, victims of a great injustice, were powerless to right the wrong committed against them. When Jack Masterman arrived in the fishing village of Penderow, he vowed to get justice for the Deverals. But the guilty parties were ruthless in protecting their interests. Meg and Jack faced murder, abduction and a desperate race against time before they could finally admit that, in each other, they'd found the one true light of their life.

JANET WHITEHEAD

LIGHT OF MY LIFE

Complete and Unabridged

LINFORD
Leicester

First published in Great Britain in 2012

First Linford Edition
published 2013

Names, characters and incidents in this book are
fictional, and any resemblance to actual events,
locales or organizations, or persons living or dead
is purely coincidental.

British Library CIP Data

Whitehead, Janet, *1958 –*
    Light of my life. - - (Linford romance library)
    1. Love stories.
    2. Large type books.
    I. Title II. Series
    823.9'2–dc23

    ISBN 978–1–4448–1471–2

Published by
F. A. Thorpe (Publishing)
Anstey, Leicestershire

Set by Words & Graphics Ltd.
Anstey, Leicestershire
Printed and bound in Great Britain by
T. J. International Ltd., Padstow, Cornwall

This book is printed on acid-free paper

For Sarah Quirke

1

'Oh . . . fiddlesticks!'

Breathing hard, Meg Deveral stood back from the patch of clay soil she'd just been trying to break up with her father's rusty old fork. The garden at the back of the ramshackle cottage was a sight, and she'd been hoping to do something with it, but it seemed that the heavy, stubborn soil had other ideas.

Before she and her father had moved in, the crooked little cottage in the middle of Olvey Row had lain deserted for two years, and in that time the garden had run riot. The cottage itself hadn't been so bad, and by the time they'd moved in their few modest sticks of furniture it had looked almost homely. Still, Meg had known it would never replace the home they had so recently lost.

That being the case, she'd turned her attention to the garden, thinking that if she could make something of that, maybe she could put her own seal on the place and find some measure of peace, or at very least acceptance. But it was difficult to know where to begin.

It had come to her the previous evening that since it was now the beginning of autumn, it might be a good idea to plant some gooseberries. And so, first thing this morning, she had gone out into the weed-choked garden, selected a sunny, sheltered spot beside one of the crumbling red-stone walls and set about breaking the soil into clods.

Unfortunately, the soil was heavy and of poor quality; she doubted that her plants would thrive there anyway.

Still, she had to try. So she kept digging deep and struggling to turn the unwieldy earth, until finally the fork went into the ground and refused to pull back out.

Meg tugged on the handle, a strand

of rich, naturally kinky auburn hair spilling down across her flushed forehead as she did so, but she must have thrust the implement in harder than she realized, because it remained stuck fast — hence her frustrated cry of, 'Oh . . . fiddlesticks!'

She had no idea how long the man had been watching her until he finally said, 'Hard work.'

Startled, she turned and saw him standing at the corner of the cottage, where a narrow, shady dogtrot that separated them from their neighbours led back toward the downward-sloping lane itself. He was tall and sturdy-looking, with thick, nape-length black hair and a pleasant, weather-beaten face. He hooked a thumb over one broad shoulder and said, 'I *did* knock, but there was no answer.'

He seemed friendly enough, but Meg was immediately on her guard. She had never seen the man before and had learned — the hard way — to be wary of strangers.

'It could have been that no one was home,' she replied stiffly.

His smile was a disarming flash of white teeth against burnished skin. 'Oh, I knew someone was home,' he said. 'I heard you cursing, Miss . . . Deveral, is it?'

Meg felt herself blushing. 'I'd hardly call 'fiddlesticks' cursing,' she said.

'Of course not,' he replied mildly. 'Just my joke, miss.' He gestured to the fork. 'You look like you're having trouble there. Can I help?'

Without waiting for a reply, he strode across to her. He was about thirty, and at an even six feet a good seven inches taller than she. He wore black canvas work trousers tucked into stout hessian boots, and a collarless white shirt beneath an unbuttoned pea jacket. She thought he might have been a fisherman she had never seen in Penderow before, for he certainly had the look of the sea about him.

He closed one large hand around the fork handle and made short work of tugging it free. 'There you go,' he said.

'Thank you.' She took the fork back from him. 'You have the advantage of me, Mr . . . ?'

'I apologise, miss,' he replied. He had a strong but gentle voice. 'My name's Jack Masterman, and I'm new to the village. They told me in the high street that you take in washing.'

'I do,' she replied. 'I charge sixpence a bag — and sixpence more if you want your things ironed as well.'

'I'll need both.'

'Did you bring anything with you, Mr Masterman?'

'I thought it best to enquire first. In any case, we only arrived late yesterday afternoon. I've come to take charge of the lighthouse at Penderow Point.'

At the mention of the lighthouse, her attitude toward him cooled instantly, and he saw as much in the anger that flared without warning in her amber eyes.

'I'm sorry, miss,' he said with a frown. 'Did I say something wrong?'

'I think you had better leave,' she replied, her voice now low and clipped. 'And I'll thank you to find someone else to do your washing.'

'But I don't understand — '

'And I have no obligation to explain,' she bit back sternly. 'Now leave, if you will.'

He looked down at her, puzzlement plain on his even-featured face. But he saw by the firm line of her mouth and the steel in her eyes that there was nothing to be gained by trying to understand her behaviour. He took a step back from her and dipped his head respectfully.

'As you will, miss,' he said, his voice still soft and polite. 'I'm sorry if I've caused you any distress. I didn't mean — '

'Just go!' she said, and he was startled to see tears spring to her eyes.

He held back briefly, then turned and strode away. She watched him leave, her lower lip quivering, and when he finally vanished around the corner of the cottage she gave vent to her feelings and slammed the fork back into the ground, then lifted her coarse woollen skirt and hurried back into the cottage.

She crossed the kitchen's flagstone floor and halted in the parlour doorway. Her father was snoring softly in the chair by the hearth.

She looked down at him. Perhaps it was just a trick of the light, but all at once he seemed so small and old and frail, as if something vital had been wrenched from him ... which she supposed it had.

Yet again she felt the injustice of it all boil up inside her and clenched her small fists impotently, not knowing what she could possibly do to deal with it or make everything better.

She returned to the open back door. There she once again stared out at the garden. It was more like a jungle, such a far cry from the orderly little plot she'd grown up with.

Angrily she tried to pull herself together. She was nineteen now, and no longer a child. Besides, she had to be strong for her father. He had been no less devastated than she by what had happened, but he had set his own feelings aside in order to be there for *her*. The least she could do now was be equally as strong for him.

Suddenly she heard the hearthside chair creak and stiffened as her father, Ennor Deveral, shuffled into the kitchen to join her.

'Everything all right, *douter?*' he asked around a yawn.

Without turning to face him she said briefly, 'Aye, Da'. Fancy a cup of tea?'

But her voice betrayed her. He heard the choked quality to it and said, 'You been *crying*, lass?'

It was on the tip of her tongue to say no, but he knew her as well as she knew him. 'Oh, it's nothing,' she said instead, trying to make light of it. 'Just tired, I 'spect.'

He came closer, reached for one of her arms and gently turned her to face him. He was only in his early fifties but he looked so much older, and the revelation did nothing to lift her mood. When she was a child he'd been like a giant to her, always ready to scoop her up and spin her around until she screamed with delight. They'd always been close, and after Meg's mother died they'd grown closer still. She loved looking after him. But the events of the past few weeks had taken a heavy toll on him, and he was now but a shade of his former self.

'Come on, now,' he said gently, and gave her a hug. His bald head was surrounded by fine white hair, his deep-lined forehead leading down to still-dark eyebrows. The eyes themselves were dark and still capable of showing mischief, his nose big, his cheeks hollow, his thin lips enclosed by a shaggy white beard. 'What's wrong, lass?'

'The garden,' she hedged. 'I don't know where to begin.'

He held her at arm's length and cocked his head at her. 'Is that *all* it is?' he asked doubtfully.

She sagged and looked away from him. 'There was a man here, just now,' she said at last.

'Oh?'

'The new lighthouse keeper.'

He considered that, then said, 'What happened?'

'He wanted me to do his washing.'

'And what did you tell him?'

'When I found out that he'd taken your job — '

'It's not my job anymore, lass.'

'Well . . . I told him to look elsewhere.'

'In other words,' he said, 'you sent the poor fellow away with a flea in his ear.'

He looked at her a moment longer, then shook his head, and all at once he was the giant she remembered and she was a little girl all over again.

'You've got to put it behind you, lass,' he said softly. 'I know I disappointed you — '

'Of course you didn't.'

'I disappointed *myself*,' he went on, as if she hadn't spoken. 'But what's done is done, and as near as I can see, there's no *undoing* it. But one thing's for certain, Meg. It wasn't the new keeper's fault.'

'Maybe not.'

'There's no *maybe* about it, *douter*. He's not so different to me, whoever he is. He's a working man and he goes where he's told to go and does what he's paid to do. You can't hold him responsible for something that happened long before he'd even *heard* of Penderow.'

He was right, of course. She'd been wrong to take it out on Jack Masterman. He hadn't been responsible for any of their misfortunes. He hadn't even known who she was! She remembered the puzzlement she'd seen in his eyes — as gentle blue as sea holly in early June — and felt a stab of guilt. He'd been pleasant from the first, friendly by nature, she thought. And yet she had sent him packing as if he were nothing more than a common vagabond.

'You'll have to go and apologise,' her father said.

'Oh, he'll have forgotten all about it by now,' she replied, going across to the copper kettle. 'Probably hasn't given it another thought.'

'No,' he agreed, 'he probably hasn't. But it's the right thing to do, *douter* — apologise.'

He was right about that, too. But then, he had always been easy-going and mild-mannered, ready to forgive and forget, and she had envied him that. In that respect she took after her mother in her often-impetuous ways.

'It means having to going back to the Point,' she said. 'That'll be hard.'

'Aye,' he replied, 'but it won't kill you, lass. You're stronger than you think.'

'I'll make us a cup of tea first,' she decided.

'And then . . . ?' he prodded.

She offered him a tremulous smile. 'And then I'll go and make my apology,' she conceded in a small voice.

12

2

She was as good as her word.

As soon as they'd finished their tea Meg draped a plaid shawl around her shoulders, left Olvey Row behind her and walked slowly up towards the high street.

Penderow was a remote, tightly-packed little village built in tiers across a sloping granite cliff that overlooked a picturesque fishing harbour and the slate-grey Celtic Sea beyond. The cobbled streets were all pitched either uphill or down dale, but the views were breathtaking.

Beyond the horseshoe-shaped harbour below, the sea stretched toward a gently-bowed horizon, where it met a cloud-streaked sky the same pale blue as a robin's egg.

Nearer to hand, laughing gulls floated and wheeled directly above the anchored fishing fleet, constantly on the lookout for scraps. A cool breeze blew straight in off the Atlantic to pluck at Meg's shawl and stir the sea into a million white-tipped wavelets.

As she passed the last of the small village shops, she tried to prepare herself for her first look at the old place after so long. It was an emotional moment for her.

A few minutes later lighthouse came into sight around a curve in the rutted, tree-lined path, and she slowed to admire it.

The lighthouse, known as Penderow Point, was a tall, sleek-looking white-washed shore station. Its tower, into which small, black-framed windows had been set at regular intervals, led up to a watch room that sat directly below the service room. Black iron railings marked the position of the narrow, so-called 'widow's walk' above that, beyond which she could make out the latticework of glittering storm panes that protected the all-important lantern room itself.

The tower was finished off by a

domed, copper-clad roof with a tall, ball-ended lightning-rod.

Her throat immediately tightened. She felt that she knew every brick of the place, every one of the 204 steps in its circular staircase.

An old brownstone cottage with a red tile roof and small white-framed windows sat in the shadow of the tower. Until recently this had been the only home she'd ever known, and it still didn't seem right to her that it was now home to someone else.

But again she tried to pull herself together. It was as her father had told her. *What's done is done, and as far as I can see there's no undoing it.* If he could accept it, then so could she.

But it was difficult. There were so many memories attached to the place, and it seemed to her in that moment that every single one of them came back in a rush to bedevil her; the innocent fun of her childhood . . . the laughing mother who was no longer here . . . the giant her father had once been, now reduced to a shade of his former self . . .

Despite her best efforts to avoid them, tears swamped her eyes. The fingers of her right hand twisted into the material of her shawl and she realised suddenly that she couldn't do this, not right now. Even just seeing the place again from a distance was too painful.

She was about to turn and retrace her steps back through the village when her attention was taken by a little girl, who came walking around the side of the lighthouse from the direction of the little storage shed, carrying a rag doll in her arms.

Because it was the last thing Meg had expected to see, she forgot all about her own troubles and simply watched for a moment, seeing not this little girl, but the little girl she herself had once been.

The child was about eight. She wore a pale brown flannel dress with a full skirt, and flat black shoes. Her hair was long and fair, worn in a series of corkscrew curls, and her clear skin was coppered by the summer sun just gone. She was chattering away to the rag doll, and though Meg was too far away to hear what was being said, she could well imagine. She had chatted away to her own dolls in much the same way at that age.

She suddenly realised that the little girl had glanced up and spotted her. Now the girl came across the tufted grassland that fronted the lighthouse, her green eyes wide with interest.

'Hello!' she called.

Meg smiled down at her. 'Hello.'

'Why are you crying?'

'I'm not.'

'Your eyes are all wet.'

To change the subject, Meg said, 'Do you . . . uh, live here?'

The girl nodded. 'We only moved in yesterday.' She squinted up at Meg. 'Do you live in the village?'

'Yes.'

'I'm Ellen,' said the little girl. 'Ellen Masterman. Who are you?'

'I'm Meg Deveral.'

'This is Chloe,' said the little girl, lifting the rag doll up.

'Hello, Chloe,' said Meg, playing along with her. 'I'm very pleased to meet you. I love your dress.'

Ellen smiled. 'Chloe says thank you.'

'Well,' said Meg, casting another uneasy look at the lighthouse. 'I should really be on my way . . . '

The girl looked disappointed, and that summoned another memory for Meg. She had loved this place, but its location, set as it was midway between the village and Bane House, which was further inland, could sometimes make her feel isolated from her friends. More than once she had had to make her own amusements here.

'Will you come again?' asked Ellen.

'Oh, I should think so. Well, goodbye, Ellen. Goodbye, Chloe.'

'Going so soon?' called a new voice.

Jack Masterman had come out of the lighthouse, wiping his oily hands on a piece of old sailcloth. He came across to them and smiled down at Meg as if he had indeed forgotten all about the unfair way she'd treated him just a couple of hours earlier.

'This is Miss Deveral,' he said to Ellen.

'*I* call her Meg,' said the little girl.

'Oh, you do, do you?' He looked at Meg, who felt herself blushing beneath his appreciative scrutiny. 'Would you like to come in for a moment, Miss Deveral? I'm just about to make a cup of tea.'

'No, I . . . I won't stay. I just . . . '

'Yes?'

'Well . . . ' She squared her shoulders and lifted her chin. 'I believe I treated you rather unfairly earlier today, Mr Masterman, and I wanted you to know that I'm sorry. My mind was . . . elsewhere, I suppose, and I was feeling snappish.'

'You don't have to apologise,' he replied. 'The fault was mine, miss. I didn't realise who you were until I got talking to someone in the village afterwards. When they let it slip that you used to live here — '

Ellen's eyes widened at this revelation. 'Did you *really* used to live here?'

'Yes,' Meg confirmed, 'I really did.'

'Well,' said Jack, 'I realised the mistake had been mine, and I was going to come back down to Olvey Row later today and apologise to *you*.'

'You have nothing to apologise for,' Meg assured him.

'Then we can start over with a clean slate,' he replied. 'Are you sure you won't come inside for a cuppa?'

'I'm sure. I just wanted you to know . . . well, if you still need your washing and ironing done . . . '

'I do indeed,' he nodded. 'If it's agreeable, I'll fetch a batch down to you later this afternoon.'

'Oh, please stay,' said Ellen. She looked up at her father. 'Are you hungry, Dad? Shall I get the bread and cheese out?'

He smiled down at her and tousled her head affectionately. 'Go on, then,' he said. 'But don't touch any knives.'

The girl ran off to perform her task. They watched her go, and then Jack said, 'Well, I appreciated you coming up here. I don't suppose it was easy for you.'

'What makes you say that?'

'Because you've been crying, miss,' he said simply.

'No I haven't. I . . . ' She deflated suddenly and said, 'Yes. Yes, I have. Silly, isn't it? A grown woman crying like a little child.'

'It depends on what you've got to cry *about*, I suppose.'

She shrugged and turned to face the sea. 'I daresay you've heard what happened. I mean, why Da' lost his job.'

'I've heard what people have had to *say* about it,' he replied. 'Maybe it's about time I heard the truth of it.'

'Don't you believe you already have?'

'It's always been my experience, miss, that there are two sides to every story. I'd hear yours, if you'd care to tell it. Besides . . . '

His voice trailed away.

'Yes, Mr Masterman?'

'Call me Jack,' he said. And then: 'Well, I get the notion it would do you good to tell it. To unburden yourself, so to speak.'

As she considered that, he gestured toward an old deadfall log that had lain in the tall grass for as long as she could remember. Years before, her father had planed down the top to make a rough-and-ready bench. Together they went over to it and sat down.

She said nothing immediately, but she realised that he was right. She had kept everything bottled up inside her for so long. There really hadn't been anyone to tell, after word got around. She and her father had become out-casts, or as close as made no difference. And maybe that's why she had allowed the burden to drag her down and poison her heart — because she'd had no choice but to allow the wound to fester inside her.

'It's a short enough tale to tell,' she

said after another moment. 'My father served this community well for nigh on twenty-five years. But then one evening about three months back . . . well, two men he'd never seen before — travellers who were passing through, they said — came to our door, seeking shelter. It was a wretched night and blowing a gale.

'There was no way Da' would leave them out there in such a storm. The men seemed friendly enough, and after a time produced a jug of ale. Da' only took a drink out of politeness, but . . . well, we realised later that they must have put something in it, a sleeping-draught or the like, to knock him out.'

'Where were you while all this was going on?' asked Jack.

'I was away in Trelaske at the time, visiting my mother's brother and his wife.'

'I didn't mean to interrupt. Go on.'

'Well, there isn't really much more to tell. Da' passed out and the men doused the light, and because of that a ship, the *Persephone*, foundered on the rocks below.'

'The Devil's Teeth,' he muttered softly, his eyes automatically moving to a point beyond the ragged cliff-edge, below which a line of treacherous rocks with needle-sharp points thrust up from the bottom of the sea.

She nodded. 'Sometime during the night the *Persephone* was looted of all her cargo and three of her crew — three who survived the initial wrecking — were shot dead by the thieves.'

'And people said your father was in on it.'

'The board of inquiry couldn't prove he was in league with the wreckers, but neither could *we* prove that he wasn't. So the only thing they could do was charge him with dereliction of duty and take the job away from him.'

'And give it to me,' he replied gently.

'I was wrong to hold that against you,' she said. 'Da' said so, and he was right.'

'Your Da' sounds like a decent man,' he said, 'and one I should like to meet. Perhaps when I fetch my laundry . . . ?'

Meg summoned a smile. 'I think he would like to meet you, too. We . . . well, it's as I said. A great many of the villagers felt as if we had betrayed them, and they turned their backs on us. Friends have been few.'

'Well, thank you for coming,' he said. 'I appreciate it.'

'I'm glad I did,' she replied, and was surprised to realise that it was true. 'You have a lovely little girl, Mr Masterman. You and your wife must be very proud of her.'

A nerve twitched in his cheek and it seemed to her that he was seized by a sudden restlessness. 'My wife's gone,' he said quietly.

She studied his profile as he looked gravely out to sea. 'I'm sorry,' she said.

An awkward silence settled between them, and she rose. 'I'll, ah . . . expect you this afternoon, then,' she said.

He nodded, recovering himself. 'Aye,' he said. 'I'll see you then, Miss Deveral.'

'Oh, Meg, please.'

'Meg,' he repeated, brightening again. 'And I'm already looking forward to it.'

3

Later that afternoon Jack Masterman and Ellen came to visit. It had been so long since anyone had shown them friendship that Meg felt her heart leap when she glanced out the tiny front window and saw them coming through the gate.

'They're here, Da'!' she cried, and immediately set about giving their poky little parlour a last-minute tidy-up.

From his hearthside chair, Ennor watched her with a rare smile lighting his face. 'For heaven's sake, *douter*, the man's only coming to drop off some washing!'

'I just want to make a good impression, that's all,' she replied with a blush. 'I was very unfair to him when all he showed me was kindness.'

'All right, Meg, all right. I believe you — thousands wouldn't.'

'And what is *that* supposed to mean?'

she demanded with hands on hips.

Before he could reply there was a brisk rapping at the door. She gave the front of her maroon dress one final smooth, then went to answer it.

A short time later Jack had deposited his little sack of washing in the kitchen and was shaking hands with Ennor. To Ennor's delight, young Ellen offered him a curtsey and a clear, well-mannered, 'Very pleased to meet you, Mr Deveral.'

'And I to meet *you*, young lady,' he replied. Gesturing to another chair he added: 'Make yourself comfortable, Mr Masterman — '

'Jack.'

'Well, make yourself comfortable, Jack, while the girls go and make the tea. My Meg has been a whirlwind ever since she got back from the old place, whipped up a saffron cake that's still warm from the oven!'

'Da'!'

As Meg and Ellen went into the kitchen, Ennor studied the new light-house keeper. Jack was big and sturdy, with a straight, unflinching stare — he'd do a good job up at the Point, Ennor decided, and immediately added, *Better than I did, at any rate*.

Remembering that fateful night, Ennor dug an old clay pipe from the pocket of his unbuttoned waistcoat and said, 'Meg tells me she told you all about, ah, what happened. I mean, how I came to lose *your* job.'

'Aye, Mr Deveral — '

'Ennor.'

'Aye,' Jack continued. 'And for what it's worth, I believe her, just as I believe you.'

'It's kind of you to say — '

''Tis nothing to do with kindness, Ennor. You've raised that girl well, and she's as loyal to you as my Ellen is to me. You look into Meg's eyes and you can see the honesty in her. I see that same honesty when I look into *your* eyes. If Meg says that's the way it happened, well . . . that's good enough for me.'

Over the past few months Ennor had

grown so used to hostility that this sudden declaration of trust made him swallow hard and fuss unnecessarily with his pipe. 'I wish there were more like you, that's all I can say,' he managed at last, his tone gruff.

'Who knows?' said Jack. 'Perhaps between us we can change a few minds.'

'Wait until you've been here a bit longer, lad. You'll soon see that that's easier said than done.'

'Even so, Ennor . . . '

Ennor frowned at Jack's tone. 'What?'

Jack sat forward and said earnestly, 'I've heard stories on my travels. Stories not so very different from yours.' He eyed the older man carefully for a moment, then said, 'This has happened before, you know. Not around here, but at Castletew, Molmoor, Little Shayle and a few other places. Not exactly the same way, of course, but close enough . . . and so spread out over the last three or more years that few people have made the connection between them.'

Ennor's watery blue eyes saucered.

'Then we've got to let the board of inquiry know! This could prove my innocence!'

'Not so fast, man,' cautioned Jack. 'We can certainly prove it's happened before. But how can we prove it happened here, to *you?* Who's to say you weren't in league with the wreckers?'

'But you just said — '

'I said I believe you. And I *do*. But boards of inquiry don't judge a man by what they see in his eyes. They demand proof. Evidence.'

Ennor looked crestfallen. 'There isn't any.'

'Maybe not,' the younger man allowed. 'But I've been thinking. There's a gang at work here, Ennor. They're well-organised, and they know what they're about. But nobody's perfect. If we could find even the smallest thing to support your version of events, Trinity House would have to give you the benefit of the doubt and open the case up again.'

Ennor struck a match and lit his pipe. 'They're organised, all right,' he replied. 'It wasn't any coincidence that they turned up here that night. They knew I'd be all by myself, and they knew the *Persephone* would be passing through.'

'So they're local.'

'Most likely. But they're dangerous, as well, lad. A lot of men died that night, and not only from the wreck. More than one was finished off with a bullet.'

'Well, I've no wish to catch one of *those*,' Jack returned grimly. 'But I reckon I'll have a nose around, anyway.'

Meg and Ellen fetched in the tea-things, and then Meg disappeared upstairs to her own small bedroom, to return a few minutes later carrying a handsome wooden doll with pegged joints, wearing a slightly dusty burgundy-coloured dress.

The doll had a composite head, which had been moulded from pulped wood and then painted. Its skin was pale, its expression somewhat sober, its sausage curls an appealing shade of yellow. It had been Meg's favourite toy when she was Ellen's age, and the minute Ellen set eyes on it, she was just as captivated.

'Ooh, she's lovely!' she said.

'Take her,' smiled Meg. 'Her name's Polly — and she's yours now, if you want her.'

The girl's mouth dropped open, but she hesitated before reaching for the toy and looked at her father. 'Can I, Dad?' she asked uncertainly.

Jack grinned at her. 'Just as long as you remember to say — '

' — *thank you!*' said Ellen, taking and hugging the doll. 'I'll love her forever, and so will Chloe!'

'I remember you were having some trouble with the ground out back,' said Jack, taking a cup of tea and a slice of warm saffron cake. 'If you need any help with digging, you only have to ask.'

'Oh, no, I couldn't — '

'It's no trouble, Meg. I'd be happy to

do it. And by the way, Ennor, while I think of it, that lighthouse is a credit to you. I've seldom seen one that was better looked-after.'

Ennor shrugged modestly. 'She was good to us, lad. It was no hardship to lavish attention upon her.'

They passed a very enjoyable hour. It was as if they'd known each other forever. While Jack and Ennor swapped stories about the light-keeper's life, Meg found an old story-book she'd kept from childhood and Ellen snuggled up beside her on the bench-sofa with Polly in her arms, and hung on every word Meg read to her.

Sometime later Jack glanced up at the little tin clock on the mantelshelf and said, 'I noticed a fine-looking alehouse in the village. It was called the Peacock. I wonder if you'd let me buy you a drink, Ennor?'

Again the older man looked at him with something akin to wonder. But: 'Better not, Jack,' he said after a moment. 'You won't win many friends hereabouts if folks see you drinking with me.'

'That's all right,' said Jack, smiling easily. 'Friendship should be *given*, not *won*.' He stood up. 'Now, are you coming or not?'

Though Ennor was tempted, he shook his head. 'Folk haven't really given Meg or me the time of day since the wreck, and it gets lonely when you're made to feel like an outsider, especially in a place that was once so welcoming to you. No one likes us much now, Jack.'

Before Jack could reply, Ellen stopped playing with her new doll and looked very seriously into Ennor's face. '*I* like you, Mr Deveral,' she said.

Ennor's face softened as he looked down at the girl. 'And I like *you*, little princess,' he said huskily.

But Jack, his mind still elsewhere, was scowling. 'If these folk are that shallow, they're not worth knowing.'

'Maybe not. But if you won't think of yourself, lad, think of young Ellen here.

She'll have to pay the price as well, you know.'

That obviously gave Jack food for thought. 'She's got no one save me, not since her mother went,' he said quietly. 'We've no family, Ennor. And living the way we have, we've never been in any one place long enough to make real friends.'

'All the more reason not to ruin the chance she's got to make some *now*.'

Jack nodded. 'Fair enough. But it might be that we can use this to our advantage.'

'How so?'

'Could be I'll learn more about this business alone.'

'Leave it, Jack,' said Ennor. 'It could get nasty.'

'That's a chance I'll take,' Jack replied, and nodding toward Ellen said, 'If you'll give eye to your new little friend, here, I think I'll go and see what I can find out at the pub.'

4

As darkness fell that evening, Ned Magowan left his tumbledown cottage in Tredray Lane and reluctantly turned his steps toward Beechy Meadow, which lay some three miles north of Penderow.

MacGowan didn't normally go up to Bane House unless he was summoned, and he preferred it that way. There had always been something about the Bane brothers, Talan and Cador, that unnerved him.

The Banes were an old Cornish family, with a long, proud history. They had initially amassed their wealth as merchants during the reign of Henry VIII, and been ardent royalists during the English Civil War. In later years, Sir Kenwyn Bane had served with distinction as a Conservative Member of Parliament and High Sheriff of Cornwall.

His son, Tristan, had continued his father's good work in politics and was eventually raised to the peerage. Even here he continued to occupy various positions of power and influence, and discharged his duties with diligence and honour.

But when he died, his sons Talan and Cador had taken over the estate, which was some 10,000 acres in size, and there the illustrious line had ended.

Put bluntly, the brothers were profligates and wastrels. Born to privilege, they had never understood the need to work or consider their responsibilities to others. It was said that Tristan's wife, the weak-spirited Hazel, had catered to their every whim and in the process spoiled them beyond redemption.

Ned Magowan believed it.

The brothers were arrogant and selfish in the extreme. They had squandered the family wealth and brought shame upon the family name. They were almost universally despised, but in equal measure they were also feared, for they had vile tempers, the pair of them, and Ned knew them both to be capable of —

But he curtailed that particular thought.

He knew what they were. He'd known what they were when he'd thrown in with them, God help him. At any other stage in his life, he wouldn't have even given them the time of day. But they'd caught him when he was desperate, when his poor Hilda had been struck down with typhus, and he'd needed money to try and cure her, or at least ease her suffering.

Of course, the irony was that in the end Hilda had died anyway. But by then he had already submitted to the Banes, and there could be no walking away from them after that. They knew too much about him, and he about them.

Now Ned trudged along a narrow, uneven country lane that was edged in on both sides by bare-branched alder and silver birch, spindle and black-thorn. He felt wretched. He knew he had made a terrible mistake, taken a wrong turning somewhere in his life that had led him to the sorry state in which he now found himself. And yet here he was, traipsing up to Bane House to report to the brothers just like the good little puppy-dog he was.

He hoped the Banes would reward him for the information. They wouldn't give him much, of course, but perhaps enough to buy himself another bottle of rum with which to drink himself into oblivion.

And yet it had been something else that had prompted him to make this hike — fear.

The sky darkened and the moon rose, painting the countryside in chilly shades of white and silver. Alongside him, creatures scuttled through the brittle undergrowth and bats flitted erratically overhead. It was as if the shadow-thick countryside had suddenly come to life and its every nocturnal occupant had come out to watch him.

All at once the village seemed a long,

long way behind him.

At length his feet began to crunch on the long gravel path that led to Bane House. It stood as a large black rectangle in the distance, with butter-yellow light spilling from just two or three of its tall, narrow ground-floor windows.

It had once been a magnificent Tudor-style house with prominent cross gables and tall chimneys set into its steeply-pitched roof, and it had been surrounded by natural gardens that had long-since run wild. Once, the front of the house had been embellished by climbing plants such as wisteria and roses. Now their last dead remnants clung sadly to the walls in various shades of dead, dry brown.

Ned felt his heart begin to race as he approached the place — stupid, he knew. He'd been here enough times in the past and should be used to it by now, but he'd never enjoyed the experience.

As their fortune had dwindled, so

Talan and Cador Bane had been forced to let all but one of their staff go. They had closed off much of the enormous house and allowed it to fall into neglect. But more recently they had hired contractors to start repairs, and now part of the mansion was hidden beneath a vast spider's-web of wooden scaffolding poles and tilted ladders.

Ned wanted to think that the Banes had turned over a new leaf, and were going to make something of themselves and the estate, but he did not think it any more likely than a cat barking or a dog meowing.

Yestin Treffale answered his hesitant knock. He was the only servant the Banes had kept on, a tall, heavy-featured man with a peculiar, waxy complexion. His heavy brow hung over deep-set eyes that were very dark brown. His nose was a curved beak, his thick lips sour and unsmiling. He looked down at Ned and saw a thin little man of forty, with unruly red hair and tiny, pinched features; close-set pale-blue eyes, a short nose, a narrow mouth.

'What do you want?' he asked.

Ned ran his tongue nervously across his lips. The need for a drink suddenly seemed all-consuming. 'I need to see the brothers.'

That was the way you addressed them. It was never Talan or Cador, but always *the brothers*. And you rarely ever saw one without the other.

'Why?' barked Treffale.

'I think there might be trouble,' said Ned.

Treffale considered this for a moment, then finally said, 'You'd better come in.'

He closed the door behind Ned and led him across a once-magnificent, now-shoddy lobby with a wide spiral staircase leading to the darkened upper floors. The lobby, like the name of the Banes, had long-since faded from respectability. Blank patches on the walls showed where valuable paintings had been sold off to pay the brothers' debtors. Empty spaces where tables or chairs should have stood were also missing, used to settle accounts with the Banes' many creditors.

Treffale came to a set of closed double doors and rapped briskly at one of them. A moment later a voice from inside barked a single word:

'Come!'

The butler showed Ned into a large, poorly-lit sitting room with a high ceiling. The brothers were slouched in chairs to either side of the low fire, nursing brandy glasses that glittered in the smoky lamplight. Ned came in and stood before them.

'He says there might be trouble,' said Treffale.

Talan raised one thick eyebrow. At twenty-four he was a year older than his brother, tall, spare and darkly-handsome in a sinister, predatory way. He wore his curly black hair to collar-length.

'Does he indeed?' he asked, studying Ned with dark, glittering eyes that held more than a hint of mockery. 'What's got you so worried, Ned?'

Ned cleared his throat. 'There was a man in the pub this evenin',' he reported. 'The new lighthouse keeper. He was askin' around about what happened. You know, the night of the *Persephone*. How Ennor Deveral came to lose his job.'

Cador sat forward. He was a little shorter than Talan, somewhat heavier, with a square, ruddy face topped by a mop of straw-coloured hair. 'That's only to be expected,' he said. 'He's curious.'

'It's more than that,' said Ned. 'He reckons he's heard all about the other times as well. He mentioned them.'

The brothers exchanged a look. 'What did he say?' asked Talan.

'He came in, introduced himself, bought a round or two to break the ice an' then started askin' questions about Deveral. Said as how he'd heard tell of similar things as what happened to Deveral happening elsewhere along the coast, not often, but often enough to make him think there was a gang at work.'

'He can't prove it,' Treffale growled uneasily, hovering behind Ned. 'We've

45

been too careful.'

'Aye, but what if it's more than idle curiosity?' argued Ned. 'What if he starts diggin' around?'

'Who's to tell him what he wants to know?' said Cador. He had cool blue eyes, a once-broken nose and a pitted chin. 'Aside from ourselves and Abel Keskey, we've always used outsiders.'

'But . . . I mean, if he should hear anything at all — '

'He won't.'

'But if he did, if he got the authorities to investigate again . . . well, it's the gallows we're facin'!'

Talan stood up and crossed the room so quickly that Ned actually flinched. 'Not losing your *nerve*, are you, Ned?' he demanded. 'You've done all right by us.'

'I'm not sayin' otherwise, my lord, but . . . '

'The new man's bound to be curious,' Talan went on, his voice clear, clipped, urbane. 'As for what he's heard . . . it'll all be forgotten by the morrow.

46

What happened to Deveral, it's history now. Folk have got more on their minds than raking over the past.'

He glanced at Treffale, who nodded and, without warning, grabbed Ned from behind, trapping his arms in a grip of iron and squeezing tight.

'Uhn . . . '

Talan shoved his face close to Ned's. 'But you listen up, Ned Magowan,' he rasped, his words escaping from between gritted teeth. 'Hold your nerve. Hold your nerve and remember how well you've done out of our little enterprise, how well you stand to do in all our future dealings, and just let the new man ask his questions. He'll soon get fed up when he doesn't get any answers.'

Wincing at the cruel pressure of Treffale's big fingers, Ned nodded anxiously. 'All right, my lord,' he managed, 'I'll do as you say. I just thought, what with him stirrin' up old memories, you'd want to know.'

'Well, you've told us,' said Talan, and with a gesture Treffale released his hold. 'Now get back to the village and keep your head down for a few days. There's no way anyone can touch us, provided we keep quiet.'

Ned hesitated, hoping Talan would take a coin from his pocket and slap it into his palm, but he didn't.

Ned nodded some more, feeling that it was what the brothers expected. Then Treffale put a hand on his shoulder and he flinched, but this time it was only to wheel him around and march him back to the front door. Almost before he knew it, Ned was back outside, with only the distant stars and the scuttling night creatures for company.

★   ★   ★

In the house, Cador Bane shook his brandy glass and watched the amber liquid swirl lazily. 'Well, well, well,' he said. 'What do you think, brother?'

Talan flopped heavily into his chair and thoughtfully rubbed at his stubble-darkened chin. 'I don't think we need worry too much about the new lighthouse keeper,' he said. 'But I *do* think we'd better watch Ned Magowan. He's always been too nervy for my liking. If his nerves get the better of him now and he lets something slip . . . well, he's right. It's the gallows for all of us.'

'So what do you suggest?'

'We keep an eye on him,' said Talan. He looked up as Treffale came back into the room. 'Watch him for a few days, Yestin,' he said. 'But be . . . discreet. Don't let him know you're there. Just make sure he keeps to himself and doesn't get any . . . ideas.'

Treffale frowned. 'Surely there's not much chance of that,' he said.

There was nothing of respect or subservience in his manner. The relationship between master and servant had crumbled long ago. Though they were by no means equals, they were more equal than anyone else would have expected. Treffale knew too much about what went on here at Bane House, and in his case knowledge most definitely translated into power.

'If he talks,' he continued, 'he doesn't just put a noose around our necks. He condemns himself to the gallows as well.'

'Maybe,' said Talan. 'But what if he turns King's Evidence to save his own skin?'

Treffale's heavy-featured, waxy face suddenly turned even paler, for that possibility hadn't occurred to him. 'I'll watch him,' he said in little more than a whisper. 'I'll watch him like a hawk. And at the first hint of trouble . . . '

There was no need to finish the sentence.

5

Jack Masterman's visit seemed to put new life into Ennor Deveral, and Meg was delighted to see it. Following the wreck of the *Persephone* and the verdict of the board of inquiry, it had seemed to Meg that something vital in her father had somehow withered and died. But this bright new morning he came into the kitchen with definite purpose, and announced that he was going to turn the soil in the garden so that Meg could plant her gooseberries.

'Well, have a care, Da',' she replied. 'You don't want to do yourself a mischief.'

He laughed, and she was amazed to hear it — he actually *laughed!* 'I'll give due consideration to my poor old bones,' he assured her, and went out into the blustery sunshine to get started.

Meg watched him for a time, as he

carried spade and fork to the shaded corner, stood for a while, studying the ground, then set to work. The ground was as hard and uncooperative for him as it had been for her, but there was determination in him as well today, and gradually he began to make progress.

For the first time in too long a sense of contentment came over her, and she set to work on Jack and Ellen's washing with a light heart. It was nothing short of a miracle, the change Jack's visit had wrought in her father. And shyly, even to herself, she had to confess that he had brought about a change in her, too. There was a quiet kindness to him that she had never experienced before, a confidence that calmed her and made her believe that everything really could turn out all right.

But almost at once she cautioned herself. What if he should end up believing the gossip and turning against them? It would destroy her father, and she didn't even want to think about what it would do to her.

She had enjoyed a simple upbringing. Everything in her world had always been black or white. But when the village had turned against them, when the people she and her father had always thought of as friends chose to believe the worst and not even come close to giving Ennor the benefit of the doubt, well . . . she had realised then that nothing was ever as simple as it seemed.

She remembered Jack's manner after he returned from the pub to collect Ellen. He told them that he'd asked around, casually, about the night of the wreck, but he didn't go into much detail about the answers he'd received. She knew that he'd wanted to spare her father the hurt. So he was a good man . . . but perhaps in the light of a new day he might find himself wondering if he'd been too ready to believe their side of things.

The thought dampened her mood. She had tried not to care what other people thought of them, and to an extent had succeeded. But for some reason she didn't quite understand, she realised in that moment that she cared very much what Jack Masterman thought about them.

Just then her thoughts were interrupted by a soft knocking at the door. She looked up, surprised, for callers were rare to their little cottage. Drying her hands on her apron, she hurried to the door.

A man was standing on the step, the blue eyes in his thin, pinched little face nervously scanning the downward-slanting lane to left and right. Meg frowned briefly. She had seen him around the village from time to time and knew his face well enough, but couldn't immediately place his name.

Then she remembered it: Ned Magowan.

'Yes?' she asked. 'Can I help you?'

Ned stared at her for a long moment without replying, and she was surprised by the fear she saw in his wretched expression.

'Are you all right, Mr Magowan?' she asked.

He swallowed and then blinked a few times, finally seeming to come out of whatever strange moment had claimed him. 'I'm fine,' he managed in a low voice. 'As to help . . . I'm thinkin' it's me who might be able to help *you*. But I'd want your word on it. That you'd *tell* 'em I helped.'

She shook her head, wondering now if perhaps he'd been drinking and come to the wrong house by mistake. 'I'm sorry, Mr Magowan, but I don't know what you're talking about.'

'That night,' he hissed, and took another nervy glance around. 'The night of the *Persephone*.'

Her mouth dropped open in surprise and she felt an unpleasant tingle wash across her skin. 'What do you know about that night?' she asked, and subconsciously she lowered her own voice to match his.

'Plenty,' came the answer. 'But I want your word that you'll speak up for me, when it comes to trial. You know, tell 'em to show clemency.'

Now she was completely bewildered. 'I think you'd better start at the beginning.'

But he was muttering to himself now, as if trying to get everything straight in his own mind. 'I wrote it all down,' he said. 'But I wasn't goin' to say anything. It was just for . . . you know, *insurance*. I know how to keep my mouth shut. But they think I'll break. I know they do. That's why they're watchin' me.' He suddenly looked directly at her. 'And they *are*, you know. They didn't think I'd notice, but I did. And that's what's forced my hand! If they think I'm goin' to talk, they'll do whatever it takes to stop me!'

He turned suddenly, just to check his surroundings, then faced her again. 'Anyway, I'll tell you everythin'. And in return, you'll tell 'em to go easy on me. Agreed?'

'Perhaps you should go and see Constable Hendy,' she suggested. 'Tell him everything you know.'

'No!' he replied with an adamant shake of the head. 'Without someone to stand up for me it'll be no different to puttin' the noose around my own neck. But they'll listen if someone tells 'em how much help I was. You'll do that, right? You and your father?'

She looked him directly in the eye. 'Are you telling me you had something to do with that wreck?'

'Aye,' he said, and for just a moment his pinched little face screwed up. 'God forgive me.'

'And you're willing to turn King's Evidence?'

'Why not? I'm a dead man if I don't. At least if I turn King's Evidence I have a chance to survive . . . providin' you speak for me at the trial.'

'You'd better come in,' she said, making her decision. 'We'll need to hear all about — '

But before she could say anything more he turned around quickly. Someone was coming down the broad stone steps that ran alongside the lane, and they'd accidentally sent a pebble skittering ahead of them.

As it came rolling past the gate, Ned Magowan went as white as a sheet and said, 'I've got to go!'

'No! Wait — !'

He shook his head. 'They'll kill me!' he hissed.

And then, before she could do or say anything to make him change his mind, he tore the gate open and ran down the lane, away from whoever was coming from the other direction.

Her first instinct was to go after him. If he really did have information about the night of the wreck that could clear her father, she couldn't risk him changing his mind about divulging it. But even as she took a step toward the gate she heard someone coming down the tiered steps on the other side of the high hedge and decided that she, like Ned, would sooner not risk an encounter with whoever it was. Magowan had seemed so genuine in his fear, so sincere in his belief that someone would stop at nothing to silence him, that she wondered if perhaps she and her father should worry for their own safety.

Impulsively she went back into the house, closed and bolted the door and waited. She could hear nothing now, save for her father whistling softly as he dug in the back garden. Whoever had been outside must have walked right past.

There came a loud knock at the door.

She almost jumped out of her skin. Who was it? The man Ned Magowan had been so afraid of, or Magowan himself, having summoned the nerve to come back and tell her whatever he knew?

The second rap at the door decided her. Drawing a deep breath, she pulled back the bolt and opened the door.

'Good morning, Meg,' said Jack Masterman. His smile was as broad as all outdoors, and completely disarming. Holding up a bundle he continued, 'While I was unpacking last night I found some extra sheets I'd like wash — '

'Jack!' she said, deflating; and the look on her face, as well as the tone of her voice, silenced him immediately. 'I thought — '

'Are you all right?' he asked with a concerned frown.

'Was anyone else out in the lane?' she asked. 'Did you see anyone else?'

'No,' he replied. 'Should I have?'

'There was a man,' she said. 'His name is Ned Magowan. He said he knew all about the night of the wreck and he was willing to tell everything if my Da' and me spoke up for him when it came to trial.'

'Where did he go?' he demanded.

'He heard you coming along the lane,' she said. 'He said he was being followed by someone, and he likely thought it was this man who meant him ill. He ran off just a few moments before you arrived.'

Jack considered that briefly. 'His name's Ned Magowan, you say?'

'Aye.'

'Where does he live, Meg?'

'Tredray Lane, I think.'

'I'll find it,' he said, dumping his bundle just inside the doorway. 'And then I'll have words with him.'

'You'll never find it,' she said. 'Some of these streets are worse than rabbit warrens! Wait just a minute.'

She hurried back into the house and snatched up her shawl. Then she told her father that she had to pop out quickly. Ennor looked up from his digging, ran a forearm across his glistening brow and said, 'Where — ?'

But she was already gone.

She joined Jack on the doorstep, closed the door behind her and together they walked quickly down through the village.

'What do you know about this Magowan fellow?' he asked.

'Not a lot,' was her reply. 'I thought at first he was drunk, but then I realised he was *scared*.'

'And you believe him when he says

he knows what really happened that night?'

'I'd certainly listen to what he has to say about it.'

'What does he look like, this cove?'

She described him as best she could. Jack was silent until she finished speaking. 'I noticed a fellow in the pub last night I'd describe the same way. I wonder if that was him?'

'It could well be,' she said. 'Perhaps you stirred his conscience, asking about that night . . . though it seems clear from what he said that he was more anxious to turn King's Evidence so as to avoid the hangman's noose.'

'I can't blame him for that,' he said. 'Good grief, girl, you weren't joking when you said this village was worse than a rabbit warren! I've no idea where we are!'

'We're almost there,' she said.

They had turned onto a thin, over-grown path that was little more than twin wheel-ruts worn into the long, untended grass. Skeletal trees overhung the thoroughfare and rustled dryly in the breeze. At the far end of the lane stood four little cottages, each one in a sorry state of disrepair.

'Do you know which one this Magowan fellow lives in?' he asked.

She shook her head.

Only two of the cottages were occupied. The other two were empty and boarded up. By mutual consent they went to the door of the first of the occupied ones and knocked. After a few moments the door opened and an elderly, white-haired woman who was supporting herself on a cane peered out at them through watery brown eyes.

'I'm sorry to trouble you, Mrs Gwynn,' said Meg. 'But we're looking for Ned Magowan.'

The old woman made a curt gesture with the cane. 'Last cottage in the row,' she said.

Meg and Jack exchanged a look, then retraced their steps to the gate and headed for the cottage the old woman had indicated.

It was little more than a rickety shanty. Its roof was in a poor state of repair and broken glass in the windows hadn't been replaced; the panes had just been boarded over.

They went up the weed-strewn path and once again Jack rapped his work-roughened knuckles against the door.

This time there was no answer at all.

'He's not home,' said Jack. 'Shall I try the pub? If he was as nervous as you say he was, maybe he went there for a little Dutch courage . . . or because he felt safer among other folk.'

'He's in there, all right.'

The voice made them both turn back the way they'd come, and they saw that the old woman, Mrs Gwynn, had stepped out onto her path to watch them. 'He went in there not ten minutes since,' she continued. 'I saw him scurry past my front window.'

Again Meg and Jack looked at each other. Once again Jack thumped at the door. And once again there was no answer.

'Mr Magowan!' called Meg. 'It's me, Meg Deveral! Are you all right?'

There was no response.

'He's in there, right enough,' insisted the old woman.

Jack went to one of the windows and peered through the grime. He couldn't see much . . . it appeared to be a tiny sitting-room with an easy chair . . . a table . . . and —

Suddenly he reared back from the window as if stung. Then, wordlessly, he returned to the door and put one broad shoulder to it. Meg watched him, startled, and said: 'Jack, what is — ?'

'Stay out here,' he called back, and in the very next minute the door, which was flimsy at best, splintered and shuddered inward.

Jack vanished into the cottage, which seemed dark and gloomy despite the brightness of the day. Meg waited for one brief moment; then, unable to contain her growing unease, followed Jack inside.

She drew up short in the sitting-room doorway. 'Oh!'

Jack was down on one knee, examining a body that was sprawled beside the heavy table. As he turned and looked at her, she saw the dead man's face, recognized it as Ned Magowan's and felt herself sway.

As she grasped the doorframe for support Jack hurried to her and eased her back into the narrow passage. 'Is that him?' he asked gently.

Unable to speak, she could only nod.

'It looks as if he tripped and fell and caught his head on the edge of the table,' he said. 'He's dead.'

6

She blanched and her eyes grew large in her face.

'No!'

Again she was assailed by a feeling of light-headedness, but this time he was quick to reach for her, folding his hands around her upper arms and steadying her. 'That's how it *looks*,' he repeated.

She focused on his rugged face. 'What do you mean?'

He led her back outside and called across to the old woman, who was still watching from her path with a curiosity she made no attempt to disguise. 'Did you see anyone else come past here in the last few minutes?'

'Why? What's goin' on in there?'

'Did you see anyone else?' he repeated.

'Only you two. Why?'

'No reason,' he replied. 'But Mr Magowan's had an accident. He's dead.'

The old woman's mouth dropped open in shock. '*Never!*'

'He tripped and hit his head on the corner of his table,' Jack replied. Then he said to Meg, 'Wait here — and this time I *mean* it.'

He vanished back into the house and gave the place a quick but thorough search. When he came out again he shook his head. 'I can't see anything to suggest foul play, but I can feel it in my bones.'

'Why?'

'I don't know. He comes to see you, claiming knowledge of what happened the night of the wreck. He tells you he fears for his life. He makes a run for it and when we find him again, he's dead. Now, I'm not saying he *didn't* trip and crack his head, but it's too much of a coincidence for me to swallow.'

She nodded. 'I'm afraid you're right.'

'We'd better report this to the police. You have a constable here in the village, don't you?'

'Constable Hendy,' she confirmed.

'All right,' he decided grimly. 'Let's go and tell him what's happened . . . or as much of it as we feel he needs to know right now.'

* * *

Ennor Deveral stared from Meg to Jack and back again, his expression showing just how shocked he was by the news. 'So you're saying Ned Magowan was . . . ' He hesitated, as if reluctant to use the word, then finished, ' . . . murdered?'

'We can't say for sure one way or the other,' said Jack. 'But I know what *I* think.'

He and Meg had gone straight from Ned's cottage to the little timber-fronted house in which the local policeman lived. Tom Hendy was a big-bellied man in his late forties who was happy in his work because Penderow more or less looked after itself. The constable's job usually consisted of nothing more demanding than a stroll through the village once or twice a day, often enjoying a large lunch at the Peacock and then whiling away his afternoons leaning against the harbour wall, chatting with his cronies. Aside from the wreck of the *Persephone*, and the occasional drunken altercation, life here was quiet, and that was how Hendy liked it.

So when Jack and Meg turned up on his doorstep and told him that they had found Ned Magowan dead, he was not best pleased to have to walk all the way down to Tredray Lane just to deliver the obvious conclusion.

'Poor devil,' he said with a sorry shake of the head. 'He tripped and fell and hit his head.'

Meg was about to suggest otherwise but the sudden flaring of Jack's dark eyes silenced her. Trusting his judgement, she held her silence.

They had told the constable a small white lie — that Ned had called on Meg earlier in the day to ask if she could do his laundry. Meg had noted the man's nervous manner and was worried for him. So she and Jack had gone to check on him . . . and found him dead.

Constable Hendy, craving only an easy and uncomplicated life, accepted the story without question, but when Meg finished speaking he did mutter: 'Bad luck seems to follow you Deverals about.'

Meg was used to the hostility — Jack wasn't. 'What's that supposed to mean?' he demanded at once.

Hendy offered him a withering look. He was a heavy-set man of below average height, with fuzzy grey side-whiskers. 'You're new around here,' he said. 'You wouldn't know.'

Jack was about to say more, but this time it was Meg who silenced him with a quick shake of the head. He forced himself to back down. They'd done their duty and reported Ned Magowan's death. Now it was the constable's responsibility.

Returning to Olvey Row, they told

Ennor everything that had happened. Ennor sank into his favourite hearth-side chair and swallowed hard. 'Well, that settles it, then,' he said at length. 'You can forget all about trying to take this business further, Jack. It's too dangerous.'

'But don't you *see*, Ennor? I did some asking around last night and I managed to flush someone, somewhere out of the woodwork! Which confirms two things — one, that you're telling the truth, and two — that this gang, whoever they are, really are locals!'

'Maybe. But it also proves that they're willing to kill to keep anyone from finding out the truth,' countered Ennor. 'Next time it might be you, or Meg — maybe even young Ellen, God forbid. I don't know about you, but I don't want to live the rest of my days worrying that something like that might happen. No, lad — let it go. What's done is done.'

'And the guilty parties walk free,' Jack said bitterly.

But he knew that Ennor was right. He'd stirred up a hornet's nest yesterday and already one man had paid the ultimate price for it. Maybe it was just coincidence, but more than likely he'd been silenced and his death made to look like an accident.

'All right,' he said at last. 'We'll play it your way, Ennor.'

He'd already been out far longer than he'd intended, and didn't like to leave Ellen by herself if he could help it, so he rose and said his goodbyes. At the door, he turned back to Meg and said, 'You be careful, hear me? If your father's right, and we leave things be, it'll all blow over . . . so don't fret yourself.'

'I won't,' she said. 'But you be careful, too, Jack. Whoever they are, they might be watching *you*, too, to see what *you* do next.'

'They'll find that a boring chore,' he replied with a sudden grin. 'Much as it grieves me to let it go, I'll do it — for you three.'

'Thank you,' she said softly.

She watched him turn and walk away. Just before he disappeared beyond the hedge he turned back and seemed surprised to find her still there. She raised one hand and waved shyly. He returned the gesture and then was gone.

7

Meg was convinced that she would have nightmares about poor Ned Magowan for the rest of her days, but life quickly intervened, just the way it always does.

For Meg there was her laundry and ironing to do, as well as her work in the garden as she planted gooseberries and other edibles and did as much as she could to establish her new garden. She shopped and sometimes just walked up to Penderow Point and sat for a while in the long grass to watch the changing moods of the sea, or follow the fishing fleet as it bobbed up and down on the distant horizon.

She knew that no amount of brooding would bring Ned Magowan back. The only thing she could do was try to put his unhappy fate out of her mind.

But over the days that followed she had the strongest feeling that she, just like poor Ned, was being watched.

It was nothing definite, just a curious, itchy sensation whenever she was outdoors. She would suddenly stop, wherever she was, and look around but find no one there — or no one showing particular interest in her.

And yet the feeling persisted.

Jack's job, meanwhile, kept him fully occupied. Every day he filled the wicks with oil to within an eighth of an inch of the brims, as per his official instructions. He cleaned the reflectors and panes in the lantern room to remove the residue of oil or smoke and at sunset every night he lit the lamps and kept them burning until sunrise, breaking his rest every two or three hours in order to do so.

There were two storms that week, and as they raged around the little village and sent waves smashing against the Devil's Teeth far below, he tended them all night long.

Ellen started school, but hated it. At first she wouldn't say why, but when

Jack collected her at the school gate one blustery afternoon and they walked down through the village towards the proud spire of the lighthouse, she suddenly asked, 'Do you like Meg and Ennor?'

Surprised by the question, he glanced down at her. ''Course I do. They're nice people.'

'That's not what the other children say.'

'Oh?'

'They say that Ennor's a bad man. That he did something very bad that made a lot of people very unhappy.'

'And do they say what he did to make them so unhappy?'

She shook her head.

'What do *you* think of Meg and Ennor?'

'I like them.'

'Why?' he asked.

She thought about it for a moment. 'I don't know. Because they're nice.'

'Well, I'd sooner trust your judgement than that of the other children, and for one very simple reason, lass — you *know* Meg and Ennor. The other kids don't. They're just repeating what their parents have said.'

'But why do they say Ennor's not a nice man?'

He considered that for quite a time before answering, then impulsively scooped her into his arms and continued walking. 'Something happened before we came here,' he said at last. 'There was . . . an accident. A boat smashed itself to pieces on the rocks and some people say that it was Ennor's fault.'

'Was it?'

'No, love. But sometimes people just have to blame *someone*. In this case it so happens they chose to blame Ennor.'

'That's sad.'

'Aye, it is.' He was silent for a while, then said, 'Are the other kids picking on you? Because we get along with Meg and Ennor?'

She shrugged.

'Do they?'

'They call me names,' she said at last.

His jaw tightened. 'I'll have a word with your teacher.'

'No,' she said. 'It's all right. I don't care.'

'Maybe you don't, lass, but it's wrong. Those other kids could do worse than take a leaf out of your book.'

'What do you mean, Dad?'

'They should learn to judge a person by what they *are*, not what other people *say* they are.'

But Ellen was insistent that he say nothing to her teacher about the other children, arguing that it would only make things worse for her if she was seen as a tell-tale. 'Besides, Dad,' she said, 'who wants friends like that?'

Not for the first time Jack was amazed by the level head she had on her young shoulders. But then his face clouded. She hadn't really had much choice, he remembered. Because of her mother, she'd had to grow up fast.

No more was said about the trouble at school, but when he met her the very next overcast afternoon she seemed uncharacteristically quiet and as pale as paper.

'Are you all right, lass?' he asked, concerned.

She nodded, but he could see that she wasn't her usual chirpy self.

When they got home she said she wasn't hungry and asked if she could go straight to bed. He got her tucked in and felt her forehead. She seemed a little feverish.

'You have a good night's rest,' he said gently. 'See you in the morning.'

Half an hour later he peeked in on her. She was asleep. But the last light of the autumn sunset slanted in through the thin curtains to shine off the sweat that pebbled her forehead.

He went into the bedroom, intending to use his handkerchief to dry her brow, and was startled when she opened her eyes and stared up at him.

'Dad?'

'Aye, lass?'

'I'm thirsty, Dad.'

'I'll get you a drink.'

He went to fetch a glass of water, but when she tried to sit up she winced and shook her head. 'I can't move, Dad,' she murmured. 'It hurts too much.'

'Where does it hurt, love?'

'In my tummy.'

'Just try to get some sleep. You'll feel better when you wake up again.'

The wind had picked up and the first few specks of rain started tapping at the windows. Jack left the cottage and quickly climbed to the lantern room, where he prepared and lit the lamp. When he returned to the cottage he found Ellen down on her hands and knees beside her bed, trying to clean the threadbare carpet.

'Hey, now, come on,' he said, hurrying to her side. 'Back to bed for you.'

'I'm s-sorry, Dad,' she said. 'I was sick.'

'Well, don't you worry yourself, lass. I'll see to that.'

As gently as he could he helped Ellen

back into bed. The child moved slowly, as if fearful of another attack of whatever pain ailed her. Jack tucked her in and used a damp cloth to cool the fever that was still racing through her. After a while she fell into a restless slumber, and he tried not to fret unduly. She'd probably just picked up something at school and would feel better on the morrow.

He sat with her for a while, then went back to check on the light. The lantern threw a beacon of yellow luminescence out across the choppy sea, warning any ships in the vicinity to beware of the rocks below.

It was still threatening a downpour when he returned to the cottage. Ellen was awake again, and to his alarm she was moaning softly and there were tears in her eyes.

'I'm hurting, Dad,' she managed after a while. 'My tummy's hurting.'

'All right, lass,' he said. 'I'll make it go away, I promise.'

He stroked her hair until she fell back

into a restless doze, then hurried outside and put on his jacket. The girl was clearly ill, and he felt that the best thing he could do was get the village doctor to examine her.

But even as he closed the cottage door softly behind him he realised he didn't have a clue where the doctor lived . . . or indeed whether or not Penderow even *had* one.

He glanced up at the light sweeping out toward the sea. He had a duty to maintain it, but right now he had a greater responsibility toward his daughter. He needed help — and knew where he would find it.

★   ★   ★

Meg was ironing in the kitchen and Ennor was watching her fondly from his favourite armchair, pipe clamped between his whiskery lips, when there came a frantic hammering at the door.

As Ennor rose to answer the summons, Meg said: 'Have a care, Da'.'

He nodded. Though she had told no one about her suspicion that she was being spied upon, he hadn't forgotten what had become of Ned Magowan any more than she had. Cautiously he opened the front door just a crack — until he recognised their caller.

'Jack! What brings you here on a night like this?'

'I need help,' Jack said breathlessly as Ennor let him inside. 'It's Ellen. She's poorly, and I don't know what to do for the best.'

'What's wrong with her?' asked Meg, hurrying into the narrow passage.

As briefly as he could he told them how she'd been ever since he'd collected her from the schoolhouse. Even before he'd finished speaking Meg was throwing her shawl about her shoulders. 'I'll be back as soon as I can, Da',' she said.

But Ennor was already reaching for his own coat. 'There's a storm comin', lad,' he said to Jack. 'And you can't tend to your girl and the lighthouse both.'

Jack nodded, more grateful than he could say. 'Thank you,' he muttered.

Together the three of them left Olvey Row and hurried back through the sea-facing village toward Penderow Point. The cold wind had strengthened noticeably and the persistent drizzle was steadily turning heavier.

As soon as they reached the Point, Ennor made directly for the lighthouse. Jack knew he would tend it just as faithfully as he ever had. He himself scooped up the lamp he'd left burning low on the kitchen table and together he and Meg crept into Ellen's bedroom.

Ellen was stirring restlessly, and she screwed her face up when the light filled the room and made the shadows shift.

'It's all right, Ellen,' Meg said softly. 'It's me, Meg.'

' . . . M-Meg . . . ?'

'I just wanted to see how you are,' said Meg, feeling the little girl's warm brow.

'I don't feel well,' said Ellen. 'It hurts when I try to move.'

'In your tummy?'

Ellen nodded miserably.

'Whereabouts in your tummy?'

'It hurt in the middle,' groaned Ellen. 'But now it hurts more here.' She managed to indicate her lower right side.

Meg thought for a moment, then said, 'Can I have a little look? I promise I won't hurt you.'

Again Ellen nodded.

Meg gently eased back the sheets and as lightly as she could felt the girl's abdomen. Ellen made a tiny mewling sound of discomfort, and Meg stopped. When she turned back to Jack she whispered, 'I think she might have some sort of cramp colic.'

Jack frowned. 'Is it serious?'

'I don't know. It might be. I'll go and fetch the doctor.'

'I'll go,' he said. 'It's shaping up to be a wild night.'

'Do you know Doctor Trewin's house in Sowden Street?'

'Well . . . no, bu — '

'Then I'll go,' she said, hurrying back to the front door. 'I'll be back as soon as I can.'

She opened the door and the blustery wind rushed inside, fetching raindrops with it. Before Jack could do or say anything more, she was gone, swallowed up by the stormy darkness.

8

Within moments Meg was soaked to the skin, the rain falling so hard now that she could hardly keep from flinching as it struck her exposed face. As the lighthouse fell behind her she broke into a run, splashing through puddles while thunder rumbled overhead, her only source of illumination coming from the occasional flicker of lightning.

Allowing memory to guide her, she hurried down toward the village. Around her, wind-whipped trees, their branches stripped bare by autumn, swayed and pitched like souls in torment, and beneath the howl of the wind she heard the angry waves hurling themselves against the rocks below. The boom they made sounded like cannon-fire.

The wind seemed to fight her every

step of the way. It shoved her from her path and threatened to rip the shawl from her shoulders. Bravely she fought back, stubbornly holding to her course.

Almost before she knew it she was back in the village, wet through and stumbling, drained by the effort it had taken just to get this far. She made directly for the comfortable home of Dr Trewin, praying that he was in and not out on some other call.

Bedraggled, her hair plastered to her head and shoulders, she knocked at his front door, the urgent sound almost swamped by another crash of thunder. A moment later the summons was answered by the doctor's wife, whose eyes widened in surprise.

'Goodness! Come in, child!'

Meg went inside, shoulders heaving as she tried to regain her breath. Once inside, Mrs Trewin got a better look at her, recognised her and allowed her mouth to pinch a little, as if in distaste. 'Whatever brings you out on such a night, Miss Deveral?' she asked. She was civil enough, but her tone had chilled noticeably.

Before Meg could answer, Dr Trewin himself came out of his living room, a frown creasing his round face. He was a tall, heavy-set, authoritative-looking man with a thick black beard, and thanks to his training had never been one to judge. 'Trouble, lass?' he asked with clear concern. 'Is it your father?'

Meg shook her head and explained the problem. Dr Trewin immediately shrugged into his greatcoat and snatched up the black bag that was sitting on a nearby table.

The journey back to Penderow Point seemed to take forever, but Meg supposed that was just the way it seemed. There was no conversation along the way — the savagery of the storm ensured that. At last a flash of lightning told them that they had finally reached the Point. Meg chanced a glance up at the lighthouse and saw her father's silhouette clear against the storm panes, watching them.

Jack had been watching for them too, and opened the door even as they arrived. The doctor brushed past, crossed the single room and vanished into Ellen's bedroom. Jack looked at Meg as she dripped rainwater all over the flagstone floor. He said, 'How can I ever — ?' Then he turned and fetched a towel. 'Here, dry yourself before you catch a chill.'

In her room, Ellen gave a fresh moan of pain. They both froze at the sound, fearing the worst.

A few moments later Dr Trewin came back out and said, 'You'll do me out of a job one of these days, Meg Deveral. Your guess at cramp colic wasn't far off the mark.'

Turning to Jack he continued, 'Your daughter has perityphlitis, Mr Masterman. Her appendix has become inflamed and must be removed at once.' He glanced around. 'Clear that table, if you please Mr Masterman, then scrub it down and light a few more lamps. Meg — wash your hands thoroughly and get ready to help. I can't do this by myself.'

Without hesitation Meg went to the sink and rolled up her sodden sleeves. She washed her hands and arms up to the elbows and then lit some additional lanterns while Jack cleared and scrubbed the table.

A short time later Dr Trewin carried Ellen out of the bedroom and set her down gently on the table. When the child didn't even stir Jack stared at him, his wretched expression asking the question.

'She's all right,' the doctor assured him. 'But I've administered some ether to make her sleep and a little curare to relax her muscles.'

He stripped off his jacket and rolled up his sleeves. As he washed his hands and forearms at the sink he said, 'Mr Masterman, I'll want you to take one of the lanterns and hold it steady, just a little above and to one side of my left shoulder — and no shifting it about once I start cutting. Meg — you'll do exactly as I say, when I say it. We've no time for squeamishness here, not if you want this child to live.'

Again thunder rattled overhead.

Jack held the lamp high and as instructed, making sure it illuminated Ellen well. He looked across the little girl at Meg and Meg saw tears in his eyes, which he quickly tried to blink away. She nodded and offered him a fleeting smile of encouragement.

'All right,' said the doctor. 'Let us begin. Meg — clean the lower right side of the patient's abdomen, if you please.'

Once she was finished, the doctor sighed, then set to work.

He had done this before, of course, and worked with quick efficiency. No movement was wasted as he made the first incision.

'Wipe that blood away,' he barked.

Swallowing hard, Meg did so.

The doctor carefully worked his way through the abdominal wall, dividing his attention between the site of the incision and Ellen's pale face. 'I'm now in what is called the peritoneum,' he muttered. 'And ... yes, there's the culprit.'

Meg swallowed hard and diligently followed the doctor's every order. He removed the appendix, tossed it unceremoniously into the fire and then set about stitching the little girl back up.

At last Jack whispered dryly, 'Is it ... is it done?'

Dr Trewin nodded. 'And my fine needlework is going to cost you a pretty penny,' he replied, then smiled. 'Don't look so worried, lad. Provided we keep the wound clean and give the girl enough of a chance to rest and recover, she'll be fine.'

Jack sagged with relief.

There was a soft knock at the door, and a moment later it swung open to reveal Ennor, his clothes dark with rain, his bald head and beard glistening with its drops.

'Is she ... ?' he began.

'She's all right, Da',' said Meg, sniffing.

Ennor's chin dropped to his chest

and he didn't look up again for a time. 'Thank the Lord,' he said at length. Then: 'Stay with her, Jack. I'll keep the light burning tonight.'

'Got your old job back, Ennor Deveral?' asked the doctor.

'Helping out a friend,' said Ennor. 'That all right with you, doctor?'

Dr Trewin finished stitching and tied as neat a knot as the finest seamstress. 'I'll thank you not to bite my head off,' he replied mildly. 'I only asked.'

Ennor shrugged. 'Well, perhaps it'd be as well if word of this didn't get out. There's many in this village who'd not take kindly to me coming anywhere *near* this place again.'

'And as you well know,' said the doctor, 'I'm not one of them.' He smiled again. 'Your 'secret's' safe with me, Ennor.'

At last it was done, and with the wound dressed, Jack and the doctor carried Ellen carefully back to her bedroom.

'She'll sleep now till morning and

beyond,' said the doctor. 'And when she wakes she'll feel sore and grizzly. But that'll pass. Just keep her still, and a few days from now she'll be back to her old self.'

'Thank you, doctor,' said Jack. 'I can never repay you.'

'You already have, in a way,' said Dr Trewin. 'You've restored my faith in human nature, lad.'

Jack frowned. 'How so?'

The doctor glanced across at Meg. 'By the company you've chosen to keep,' he said with a smile.

9

After Dr Trewin left, Jack flopped down into a nearby chair. The room still smelled faintly of ether; he'd open a window in a moment and air it out. For now, all he could do was sit and think about Ellen and how close he'd come to losing her.

Lord, if it hadn't been for Meg and her father . . .

He had been watching Meg as she busied herself at the sink. Only now did he realise she had turned to face him and was returning his scrutiny.

'Why don't you shut your eyes for a little while?' she suggested. 'You look just about done in.'

'I *feel* it,' he confessed. 'But I still have work to do.'

'Da' said he'd tend the lantern.'

'I mean in *here*,' he said, indicating the table and floor, both of which needed a thorough cleaning.

'I'll see to that,' she assured him. 'I've made tea. I'm just going to take a flask up to Da' and then I'll clean up.'

'I'll do it,' he insisted, climbing back to his feet. 'But I thank you, Meg, I really do. I thank you from the bottom of my heart.'

She looked up at him, realising suddenly how close they were and how intimate the moment had become. The patter of rain at the small windows and the occasional rumble of thunder suddenly faded into the background as she saw more than gratitude in his dark eyes; it was as if he were no longer seeing her as a girl but as a woman.

She flustered, brushed past him and held up the clay flask. 'I'd better get this tea up to Da',' she said. 'He hates it when it gets cold.'

By the time she returned to the cottage he had just about finished cleaning up and airing out the room and was building up the fire in the grate to chase away the chill. The storm had rumbled on to north and east by this time, and the rain was now little more than a steady drizzle.

Meg poured tea and they sat either side of the fire.

'I'm afraid I let my emotions get the better of me, didn't I?' Jack said sheepishly. 'But Ellen . . . well, she's all I have. If I lost her . . . '

'Well, you didn't,' she said. 'That's all that matters.'

Silence settled between them for a while, until Meg, unable to stifle her curiosity, said carefully, 'Does Ellen take after your wife?'

He shook his head, and then to her surprise he added before he could stop himself, 'No — thank goodness.'

He caught her look and said, 'I'm sorry if that sounds harsh. Maybe it was. But if you knew the hurt Elizabeth caused that child in there . . . '

In the light from the small fire Meg saw sadness etch his features. 'I wouldn't presume to judge you, Jack,' she promised him. 'That would make me as bad as the folk who've already judged Da' and me. Still . . . '

'What?'

'Well, she's gone now. Your Elizabeth, I mean. Best for everyone if you just let her rest in peace.'

Again his surprised her, this time with a short, mirthless chuckle. 'Is that what you think?' he asked. 'That she's dead?'

'When we first met you told me — ' Meg stopped suddenly. 'You told me she was *gone*,' she finished, realising that she had evidently misunderstood him.

'Oh, Elizabeth is still very much alive,' he told her. 'She *left* us, Meg. Deserted us.'

Meg frowned. 'How could she have done such a thing?'

'Who knows? All that matters is that she did.' He looked at her. 'Still, the fault wasn't hers alone. I had a part in it, too, I suppose.'

'How?' she asked before she could stop herself.

It was a fair question, and he paused

a while as he prepared his answer. 'When she married me she thought she was marrying a man with prospects,' he replied at last. 'I had received more schooling than most, you see, and since I could read and write and was passable when it came to figure-work, I ended up as a clerk in a firm of solicitors.

'But my heart was never in book-work. Although I was born and raised in Sheffield, I'd always had a fascination for the sea. When I was but a lad I'd set my sights on one day becoming a ship's captain, but my father had other ideas, and so it was a clerk's life for me. And it was no bad thing — the hours were regular, I had a decent enough wage, there was no call for me to get my hands dirty and, as I say, I had prospects for advancement. But it was no good. It was a life I couldn't just settle to.

'So one day I put it to Elizabeth that perhaps we could reach some sort of ... *compromise*, I suppose you'd call it. I would try my hand as a lighthouse keeper, so's I could be near the sea *and* keep my feet on dry land at the same time. If it didn't work out . . . well, I would go back to the city and find clerical work, and this time I would stick at it for her and for Ellen.

'Elizabeth didn't like it much. In fact, she made up her mind that she was going to hate it even before I got my first posting! She had ambition, you see. She'd come from even poorer stock than me and was desperate for the finer things in life, and to mix with what she always called a better class of people. And I was a fool to think she would ever change, which makes me as much to blame for what eventually happened as her.

'I took to that hard, isolated life at once. It was everything I'd thought it would be, and I loved it. After the cramped city life we'd led to that point, Ellen loved it too, the open spaces and the freedom, the birds and the sea in all her moods . . .

'But it wasn't something Elizabeth

cared for, not then, not later. In fact, she despised it.

'As the weeks went by she grew more and more snappish, and took her unhappiness out not only on me but on Ellen, and that I wouldn't stand for. I promised her I'd find another job in a big city and we'd go back to the way things were before. But by then that was easier said than done. And the longer it went on, me searching for another clerical job . . . well, let's just say that she and I grew . . . *estranged*. And she sought a measure of love and affection elsewhere.'

Meg swallowed softly.

'I didn't know anything about it at first,' he continued, talking more to himself now than to her. 'It seems daft, when I look back on it. She spent more and more time away from home, with 'friends in the village', so she said. But then I started to hear things, you know, tittle-tattle, and notice the way folk looked at me, almost as if they felt *sorry* for me.

'Well, it ended the way those things always end — with an accusation, a denial, an argument and then an admission of guilt. There was a man, she said, a merchant by the name of Benjamin Coates, who'd been staying in the village on business. They'd met each other at a tea shop and . . . what happened between them . . . it had started there.

'Anyway, this fellow Coates had to go back to Reigate and he wanted her to go with him. She wanted to go, too, no two ways about it. She was sick of me and what she took to be my empty promises.

'At first I asked her to consider Ellen. If not for any love of me, couldn't she at least stay for the sake of our child? But when I looked her in the eyes I could see that her mind was already made up, that this man Coates could give her all the money and finery and station in life she so desired; and when I saw that I told her to go and be done with it, that I alone would give our girl the love of two parents and . . . '

His dark eyes found Meg's, and found them filled with compassion.

'And,' he finished quietly, 'she went.'

'Jack,' she near-whispered, 'I'm so sorry.'

'Ah, I'm over it now,' he said dismissively. 'You may call me wicked, if you like, but Elizabeth was no loss. But for Ellen . . . well, let's just say that it hasn't been easy for her, a girl growing up without a mother.'

'Do you know what happened to Elizabeth?' she asked.

He shook his head. 'And do you know something?' he replied. 'I care even less. Does that make me evil, do you suppose?'

'It only makes you human,' she replied.

His smile turned wistful. 'If only Elizabeth had been half the woman you are,' he said sadly, 'we'd have been like characters in a fairy story, and all lived happily ever after.'

She blushed.

He drew a breath and said that he should go up to the lantern room and give Ennor a break, but Meg was quick to stop him. 'He may never get the chance to man this place again,' she reminded him. 'Let him care for it all by himself this one last time.'

He smiled in admiration. 'You've a wise head on your shoulders, Meg,' he said.

Embarrassed, she excused herself and went to check on Ellen. The girl was sleeping peacefully and her fever had broken.

When she returned to the outer room, Jack had fallen into a doze. She went through to what was now his bedroom and took a blanket from the bed, then gently draped it across him. The task done, she returned to her own chair, thought back over the events of the evening and night, and eventually fell into a shallow sleep of her own.

★　★　★

The next time she opened her eyes the milk-pale light of early morning was slanting in through the windows, and Jack was boiling water for tea. She sat forward, stretched and stifled a yawn.

'Good morning,' he said. And when she instinctively glanced toward Ellen's bedroom door he reported, 'Sleeping like a lamb.'

She stood up and dry-washed her face.

'I thought I'd make us all some breakfast,' he said. 'I daresay you and your father could use it.'

'Here,' she said, crossing to the counter beside the sink. 'I'll see to that.'

He turned as she approached him and almost before realising it, she had more or less walked straight into his arms. They bumped each other softly, and when Meg looked up at him he was staring at her with an expression she was almost scared to interpret.

'You know,' he confided, 'I'm growing to love this place, much as I daresay you and your father grew to love it. But

I'd give it up in a second if I could just prove Ennor's innocence and give him his old job back.'

Tears moved in her eyes. 'You're an uncommon man, Jack Masterman,' she said. 'There's not many who'd think that way.'

'And there's not many who'd do for us what you and your dad did last night,' he countered. 'I'm more than grateful, Meg. You and Ennor . . . you've been the closest thing to family Ellen and me have had in a long while.'

'Aye,' she said. 'And Da' and I could say the same for you.'

He looked down at her, and they were still so close that she could feel his shirt brushing softly against the front of her damp dress. She realised suddenly that she must look a complete mess, what with being out in the storm and all, though why that should matter quite as much as it did, she wasn't completely sure.

As if reading her mind, he smiled suddenly and put his hands on her shoulders. 'You know something?' he asked.

She could barely get her lips to work. 'What?' she finally whispered.

'I don't think I've ever seen a girl more beautiful than you.'

'Oh, now — '

'I *mean* it,' he said.

And she knew then that he was going to kiss her; that he felt about her the same way she, without properly realising it, had come to feel about him, and she was scared and excited in equal measure.

The room was absolutely silent. In that moment the only thing that existed for her was Jack. Her heart thumped with excitement and dread — excitement at the feel of his lips against hers, dread that he would see from her reaction that she was just a child of no experience.

He brought his head down to her raised face and his lips touched hers.

It was little more than a soft brushing at first, and as she responded so he kissed her harder — not roughly, but with unquestionable passion. His arms went around her and pulled her gently to him, and she went willingly, and with every sense swimming.

She closed her eyes and smelled his skin, felt his warmth, the first delicate probing of his tongue, and she felt in that moment that she might faint.

Certainly she never wanted the moment to end.

But at last they broke apart and she looked down at the flagstone floor, not really knowing what to say.

'I'm not much good with words,' he said quietly after a moment. 'But you must know I have feelings for you, girl.'

She shook her head and shrugged. 'I didn't really think . . . I mean, you're a wonderful man, Jack.'

'But I'm too old for you, is that it?'

'No.'

'I'm too *young* for you, then.'

She couldn't help it; she giggled.

'No. I'll tell you what you are for me,' she said finally. 'You're *perfect*.'

He was about to take her back into his arms when there came a sudden, brisk rapping at the door, breaking the moment.

He stepped away from her, cleared his throat. 'Excuse me.'

She watched as he strode to the door. It was still early, and since visitors had always been few to Penderow Point, he assumed his caller was Dr Trewin, come to check on Ellen.

But when he opened the door he revealed a woman in a two-piece burgundy suit with a black trim; and even as she watched, Meg saw the blood drain from Jack's weathered face.

'Jack,' the woman said in greeting.

And Jack said, almost in a gasp, '*Elizabeth*.'

10

Jack's errant wife swept inside without waiting to be invited. She was short and attractive, with a pale, heart-shaped face, alert green eyes, a snubbed nose and a small mouth. Beneath her matching burgundy bonnet she wore her rich auburn hair close to her head, gathered in a knot at the crown, from which it cascaded to well below her shoulders.

Meg couldn't even begin to guess how much her outfit had cost. The fully-lined cotton jacket over her buttoned-to-the-throat white blouse had fashionable three-quarter length sleeves. The full skirt fell straight to the ground, with a black cummerbund at her trim waist.

She saw Meg at once and stopped suddenly, clearly surprised. The look she gave Meg was withering.

'My,' she said, addressing Jack. 'I see you didn't waste any time moving someone in to take my place.'

Jack closed the door behind her. 'You'll keep a civil tongue in your head when you address Miss Deveral,' he replied, his voice low, tense.

Meg, as shocked by Elizabeth Masterman's unexpected appearance as Jack himself, reached for her shawl. 'I'll be going,' she said.

'There's no need,' he replied quickly. 'You're as good as family — *better*, if truth be told. There's nothing needs saying here that can't be said in your company.'

Elizabeth arched an eyebrow at him. 'Isn't there, Jack?' she asked.

Meg felt her mouth thinning. 'I'll be going,' she repeated. 'But if you should need Da' or me . . . '

He nodded, his expression grim. 'Thank you, Meg.'

He opened the door for her and she left, heading toward the lighthouse so that she could collect her father along the way.

After she was gone Jack closed the

door again, then wheeled around. 'What in the devil's name are *you* doing here?'

'That's a nice welcome, I must say.'

'What did you expect?' he demanded, wanting to shout but mindful of Ellen, resting in the other room. 'A bouquet of flowers and a marching band?'

'Now, now, Jack. Sarcasm doesn't become you.' She looked around, inspecting the cottage with clear disdain. 'I came early because I wanted to see Ellen before she goes off to school. She is *in* school, isn't she?'

'Of course.'

'Good. Education's important, especially for a girl.' She looked directly at him. 'Where is she?'

'Do you really care?'

'I won't even dignify that with an answer.'

'She's in her bedroom, resting,' said Jack, adding quickly, 'And you'll not disturb her.' He hesitated briefly, then said, 'We nearly lost her last night.'

Elizabeth's green eyes widened. '*What?*'

'She fell ill and needed an operation.

The doctor — the doctor that young girl who just left here risked pneumonia to fetch — operated on her right there on that very table.'

For the first time, Elizabeth looked uncomfortable. 'Will she be all right?' she asked.

'Barring infection, I think so.'

She looked thoughtfully at the door he had indicated, wanting to go in and see her child. Eventually she crossed and opened it, peered inside. Ellen was sleeping, her expression serene.

'What are you doing here, Elizabeth?' Jack asked when the door was closed again.

'Oh, Jack,' she said, her expression miserable. 'I've had a terrible time these past few months. It's been dreadful.'

She waited for him to ask what had been so dreadful about it, but he stubbornly refused to oblige her.

Undeterred, she continued, 'Benjamin was a brute of a man, Jack, an absolute brute! He treated me like . . . like dirt! And he . . . he beat me, too, for the slightest reason. I suffered like you couldn't imagine, and eventually resolved to leave him and come back to you, and Ellen.'

Still he made no response, until finally, 'What a tragic tale,' he said. 'Now, shall I tell you how it *really* went? Benjamin Coates got sick and tired of your selfish ways. He saw that you were nothing more than a greedy wastrel and couldn't wait to be shut of you. More than that, I suspect the fact that he was seen to be consorting with a married woman sat uneasily with his more pious customers, who started to desert him, and so he ended whatever you want to call your affair and threw you out. *That's* how it really went, isn't it?'

He saw by the way she refused to meet his gaze that he was right. Even so, she felt obliged to protest. 'That's a terrible thing to say!'

'And yet I don't hear a denial.'

'All right,' she said grudgingly. 'I'll be honest with you, Jack.'

'That'll make a change.'

'Benjamin and I . . . it was a stupid, foolish mistake, and one I regret. I allowed my heart to rule my head, and . . . ' She stopped and gave him her most beseeching look. 'I want to come back, Jack. I want to come *home*.'

'*This* is home now,' he said coldly. 'And as I recall, it's not the kind of place you'd care to *call* home.'

'But Jack — we're man and wife.'

'I may be a man,' he said bleakly, 'but you gave up the right to be called a wife the minute you walked out on Ellen and me.'

She scowled at him. 'What's become of you?' she asked. 'You never used to be bitter.'

'Don't you think I have cause?'

'I thought you would have been pleased to see me back,' she said, aggrieved. 'If not for your sake, then for Ellen's.'

'Ellen's sake!' he scoffed. 'Do you have any idea how you hurt that child when you walked out, Elizabeth? I tried to kid her on, told her that you had to

117

go back home to look after your parents because they were too old to look after themselves anymore, but she didn't believe that for a second. She knew the truth of it, and ever since you left she's done everything in her power to look after me, just as I've done as much for her.'

'Then give me the chance to make it up to her,' she implored.

'No, Elizabeth. I'll not take that chance again. It's as I said just now — this is home for Ellen and me. You'd stand it for about five minutes and then you'd start nagging at me to move back to the city again, and when I said no you'd walk out on us for the second time. And don't deny it — you know I'm right.'

She glared at him, breathing hard and fast in her rising anger. 'So I've come all this way to make amends, and you won't even give me a chance.'

'I won't give you the chance to hurt Ellen again,' he replied. 'There's a difference.'

'Then I want a divorce,' she said.

He looked at her as if she were mad. *Divorce?* Divorce was possible, of course, but almost unheard-of. Marriage and divorce were controlled by the church . . . and while the church encouraged the former, it strictly forbade the latter. The Anglican Church would allow separations, certainly, but neither spouse was allowed to remarry while the other still lived.

'I wish I could oblige you, Elizabeth, I really do,' he said. 'But divorce is beyond the reach of folks like us.'

'Then how do you expect me to make a fresh start for myself?'

'The way most other people of our station do,' he told her. 'Go somewhere nobody knows you, change your name or call yourself a widow. You're handsome enough; you shouldn't have any problems.'

'Is that what *you* intend to do?' she asked. 'With that slip of a girl I just saw?'

'I've not given the matter any

thought,' he replied honestly.

And he hadn't . . . until a few minutes earlier, when he had looked down at Meg and seen, finally *seen*, what a kind and generous, loving and selfless girl she truly was — and known beyond all doubt that whatever they felt for each other would bring them happiness and satisfaction in a way that his life with Elizabeth never could.

'Now, I think you had better go,' he said. 'And take all your foolish talk of divorce with you.'

She studied him sadly. 'I thought you would be glad to have me back,' she said.

'There was a time when I would have been,' he replied, softening momentarily. 'But that time passed a long while ago.'

Seeing that there was nothing to be gained by staying, she went to the door, and he was quick to open it for her, as if he could hardly wait to see the back of her. 'I'm booked into the inn,' she said. '*If* you should change your mind.'

'I won't,' he told her.

'Can I at least come and see Ellen again?'

'I'm not sure that'd be such a good idea,' he said. 'It would only open old wounds, wouldn't it? And when you leave you'll only hurt her all over again.'

She knew that was true, too.

'Good day, then, Jack,' she said stiffly.

'Good day, Elizabeth.'

She turned and splashed back toward the village.

* * *

Although Elizabeth had appeared to be contrite and defeated, she was actually in foul humour as she stormed off. She had been expecting a considerably warmer welcome than the one she'd received. And why not? She'd always been able to talk Jack around — it was a gift she had.

But not, apparently, anymore. He had changed since their last encounter, he seemed somehow *harder* now, less willing to take her at face value. And he had developed an intuitive streak that was uncanny.

He had been absolutely right about Benjamin. Benjamin had been completely besotted with her when they had first met, and she had basked in his adoration. He was tall and reasonably good-looking, and was a man of means and ambition. Among other business interests, he owned a large rope factory in Reigate, where he enjoyed great prominence.

He had been generous, too — at first. Even when he requested that they keep their relationship discreet, she took no offence. She understood that he had a reputation to uphold. And so she happily let him find her a charming little cottage and give her an allowance that enabled her to indulge herself to the full.

But then he had tired of her — or more correctly, he had tired of her spendthrift ways. He didn't seem to understand that money was there to be enjoyed, and not merely used as a means by which to survive. And so they had argued about it, and he had revealed a darker side to his nature than she had previously suspected.

Jack had been right about the other thing, too. Despite their best efforts to keep their relationship secret, word had eventually leaked out, and Benjamin found himself faced with a simple choice — to lose custom and continue losing it because of his relationship with a married woman . . . or to end that relationship while he still had a reputation to claw back.

She saw now that they had both been naive. It was as Jack had said — she could easily have called herself a widow and who ever would have discovered the truth in far-away Sussex? Still, it was too late now. Benjamin had bought her off with a modest sum that, he hoped, would take her far from the world he inhabited, and she had gone without complaint, confident that Jack would welcome her back, if not with open arms then at least grudgingly, and she could once again encourage him to return to the life of a clerk with prospects.

But it hadn't worked out that way, and her mood darkened still further at the knowledge.

What was she to do now? The money Benjamin had given her wouldn't last forever. Sooner rather than later she would have to rely upon herself for an income. Unless, of course, she could find —

The thought was interrupted by a coach that suddenly rattled past, sending up a great splash of muddy rainwater in its wake. At once the lower half of her dress was soaked to a darker hue, and she cried out in a mixture surprise — for she had been so deep in thought that she hadn't even heard its approach — and anger.

The coach swayed on for a few more yards, then the driver drew back on the reins and the two-horse team slowed to a halt. The driver on his high seat

124

turned around. He was a tall-looking man with a face like wax. She found him rather alarming.

Then the nearside coach-door opened and after a moment a second man stepped down. He was tall and spare, dressed well in a linen shirt with a low-standing collar, a calf-length frock coat and grey trousers tucked into tall, fitted boots. He had dark, fox-like features that were at once both predatory and, to her at least, curiously attractive.

He came towards her with a confident swagger, twirling his cane as he did so. He was, she thought, somewhere around the middle-twenties, with a deep blue tie knotted in the present fashionable 'barrel' style beneath his faintly stubble-darkened jaw.

When he was near enough he swept off his straw hat to reveal curly black hair worn to collar-length. He offered a slight bow, then studied her boldly before finally flashing his teeth in a sudden, disarming grin.

'My dear lady,' he said. 'I am so

sorry. We didn't expect to encounter anyone on the road at this early hour.'

He tilted his head and examined her curves more obviously. 'I fear we have ruined your dress,' he noted. 'A dress, incidentally, that is *almost* as attractive as the woman wearing it.'

Again he smiled at her.

She preened at the compliment, but knew better than to submit to flattery quite so quickly. 'It will certainly require cleaning,' she said, gesturing to the mud-stain.

'And I will be happy to pay the cost,' said the man. 'Provided your husband has no objections . . . ?'

He was fishing, and they both knew it. 'I am afraid my husband passed away some time ago,' she lied smoothly. 'I am a widow.'

'And you are on your way into Penderow?'

'I am, yes.'

'Then please allow me to put my coach at your disposal,' he said.

She looked at the vehicle. Whilst not

as impressive as many, it did at least hint at money, and was sure to be more comfortable than the crowded mail coach upon which she had travelled to Penderow.

While she was looking at the coach, he said, 'I am Talan Bane, by the way — *Viscount* Bane. And you are . . . ?'

She caught her breath. A viscount! She was not to know that this was merely a courtesy title dictated by tradition, or that Talan Bane had done nothing to earn it and even less to keep it. She flustered for a moment, then said, 'I am Elizabeth — ' She bit off suddenly, remembering what Jack had said. Then: 'I am Elizabeth Masterson. And I am very pleased to make your acquaintance, my lord.'

He raised one thick eyebrow, impressed. She knew the correct way to address him. She was a woman of some breeding, then, or at very least one of some education. He offered her his free arm and she took it willingly.

'Come, Mrs Masterson,' he said.

'And please — titles are so tiresome. Call me Talan.'

She simpered. 'Only if you will call me Elizabeth.'

'With the greatest of pleasure,' he said, and led her across to the waiting coach.

11

For the rest of that morning Meg tried to focus on her chores, but it was almost impossible. Too much had happened since Jack had turned up on their doorstep the night before.

To begin with, she was concerned for Ellen. Surgery had always been a risky business, of course, but the often-fatal complications that could arise from infection were only now being recognised by the medical fraternity. Jack's daughter would need no shortage of time and care if she were to recover fully from her operation.

Then, of course, there was that one single kiss — Meg's first.

She hadn't dared tell her father about it. She wasn't sure how he would react and thought he might well jump to the wrong conclusion and accuse Jack of taking advantage of her. But it had changed her whole perception of life, and made her consider her future in a new and exciting light.

She *had* told her father about Elizabeth, however. He'd seen her arrive whilst tending the lantern and was understandably curious to know who she was. After Meg had finished telling him he'd scowled, clamped his pipe firmly between his whiskery lips and announced that he had a feeling the woman was going to be trouble.

'I fear she might be at that, Da',' Meg agreed softly.

And that was perhaps her biggest worry — that Elizabeth, showing up in Penderow at just this time, would somehow become a rival for Jack's affections.

And yet as soon as the thought occurred to her she told herself not to submit to jealousy. For one thing, it was an ugly emotion. For another, she had no right to feel that way. After all, Elizabeth was still Jack's wife. They had loved each other once, and their union had produced Ellen. If Elizabeth came back into Jack's life and they rediscovered the feelings they had once held for each other, she should be glad for him.

And yet that was easier to think than to do.

Exhausted following his long, sleepless night, Ennor excused himself as soon as they arrived home and trudged wearily upstairs to sleep for a while. Meg watched him go, glad of the opportunity to be alone with her troubled thoughts.

She washed and changed out of her damp clothes, then brushed out her rain-crinkled hair. After that she forced herself to keep busy, and somehow the long morning eventually passed.

The next time she glanced at the clock on the mantelshelf she saw that it was midday. She went upstairs and looked in on her father, who was snoring peacefully under a woollen coverlet. Returning to the parlour, she quickly wrote a note telling him that she had gone back out to the lighthouse to check on Ellen. Finally she wrapped a clean shawl around her shoulders and set off back through the village.

Her nagging worry now was that she would find Elizabeth still at the Point — or worse, that she had gone one step further and actually moved in. She didn't believe that was likely, given Jack's obvious animosity toward the woman, but there was always the chance. If that was the case, Meg would simply satisfy herself as to Ellen's condition and then be on her way.

As she neared the Point she spotted Jack standing to one side of the windowless storage shed, his broad back turned to her as he chopped firewood. Immediately her heart started beating a little faster.

The day was bright but blustery, and the cold wind was coming straight in off the choppy grey sea. Hugging the shawl closer to her throat, she glanced toward the cottage, wondering if Elizabeth was in there even now, looking after the daughter she'd once abandoned, or perhaps making lunch for her husband.

The idea pricked her like the point of a knife, and once again she told herself that if that was the way it was, then she must accept it and be glad for Jack that his wife had seen sense at last and returned to him.

When she was close enough for him to hear her footsteps he turned, recognised her, set the axe down at once and came forward to meet her. As he drew closer Meg searched his face, looking for anything in his expression that would tell her how things had gone between him and Elizabeth after she'd left, but he gave nothing away.

He muttered her name in cautious greeting, and not really knowing how else to open the conversation she said simply, 'We were wondering how Ellen's getting along.'

'She woke up a little while ago, sore and scared,' he replied. 'I told her that she was safe now, and the more time she spent resting, the quicker she'd heal. But that girl's never been one for staying a'bed, and when she started getting restless I thought I was going to have problems with her.'

'What happened?' asked Meg, concerned.

'I spotted Polly,' he said, 'the doll you gave her. And as soon as she had that in her arms she settled down again and went straight back to sleep.'

'That's what she needs more than anything else right now,' said Meg, remembering that Polly had always been a comfort to her whenever she'd been poorly as a child.

Again the wind swiped at them with its cold hand, and he gestured toward the cottage. 'Step inside for a minute.'

Instinctively she balked. 'I don't want to intrude — '

'You're not intruding,' he said, and then realising what she really meant, added: 'Elizabeth's not here. She should be long gone by now.'

Meg almost sagged with relief. 'It . . . it must have come as quite a shock, seeing her again,' she commented as

134

they went into the cottage side by side.

'It did,' he confessed, adding awkwardly, 'and it made me realise how wrong I was to kiss you this morning.'

She pulled up short. 'There was nothing wrong about that,' she assured him quickly.

'There was,' he insisted. 'You see, ever since I came here I'd all but forgotten about Elizabeth. Can you imagine that, actually forgetting about the woman you married? And then, seeing her again . . . '

' . . . it made you remember how you felt about her?' she finished hesitantly. 'How you *still* feel about her?'

He shook his head. 'I have no feelings for that woman one way or the other. But seeing her again reminded me that in the eyes of the law I'm *still* married, and as long as Elizabeth lives, I can never give you the commitment you deserve.'

Her fine eyebrows pinched together in a frown, and as if from far away heard herself say, 'That doesn't matter to me, Jack. You said you had feelings for me.'

'I do.'

'And I have feelings for you, too. Isn't that enough? Surely, there's no need for anything more.'

He offered her a sad smile. 'You say that now, Meg Deveral, but just think on it for a moment. What would your father say to the idea of you throwing in with a married man? He loves you very much, Meg; he wants the best for you, and if he's even half the man I think he is, he dreams about the day he'll walk you down the aisle and see you married and settled, just as I do with my Ellen. You'll have neither of those things with me.'

'I could be *settled*,' she insisted stubbornly.

'Aye — and shunned by those around you for living in sin.'

She thought about that, but remained intractable. 'Who needs to know that?'

'No-one,' he said. 'But word, as they say, has a nasty habit of spreading. Just think what that would do for what's left of Ennor's reputation, or how the other kids would pick on Ellen because of it. Think what would happen if Elizabeth ever showed up here again and tried to make things awkward for us — or what would become of the children we had out of wedlock.'

He shook his head.

'No, Meg. Elizabeth used a phrase on me this morning that I haven't heard in a long time, but there never was a truer one, in my case. I let my heart rule my head . . . and I thank God that woman turned up when she did, and made me see sense before I ruined your life.'

She said almost desperately, 'Jack! That won't happen!'

'Maybe it won't. But I'll always be waiting for it to.'

She felt herself swaying a little and reached out for the back of a chair. 'Then we'll move away,' she said.

'No, lass. I've already considered that. But your life is here, and you'd never be as happy anywhere else.'

'What makes you think I'll be ever happy again?' she countered without thinking, and hearing the childish quality in her voice immediately apologised. 'I'm sorry, Jack. I know you only want to do what's right, but — '

'My mind's made up,' he said firmly. 'You deserve a lot more than I can give you, and in time you'll see that for yourself.'

'I won't, you know,' she assured him in a small voice.

But she knew that everything he'd wanted to say had now been said, and feeling her throat tighten with emotion she turned and started toward the door, all her dreams for the future suddenly shattered.

He reached out and grabbed her by one arm, said earnestly, 'Please don't hate me, girl.'

She looked up into his face and wanted to tell him that she could never do that, but somehow the words refused to come.

'If it's any consolation,' he continued

softly, 'I'm as sorry for myself as I am for you, Meg. Sorry that things couldn't have been different for us.'

But she barely heard him. All she wanted now was to get away from this place she had once loved so much, and this man whom she still loved and knew she always would. She slipped from his grasp, wrenched the door open and started back toward the village at a run, and behind her Jack stepped into the doorway and watched her go, knowing beyond all doubt that he had just lost the one true light of his life.

12

Up at Bane House, Elizabeth looked around the spacious bedroom she had been given and smiled in approval. This would do nicely, she thought. Very nicely indeed.

She crossed the room and sat on the edge of the four-poster bed to test the feather mattress. She found it perfect, and reminded herself just how quickly — and drastically — one's fortunes could turn. One minute she had been as close to rock bottom as she ever wanted to get, and the next . . .

She frowned suddenly. What was it that the old hymn used to say? *Though troubles assail . . . the Lord will provide.*

Well, the lord — My Lord *Bane*, in this instance — had certainly provided for *her*.

Earlier that morning, once he had

helped her climb into his coach, she had met Talan's younger brother, the blond-haired, blue-eyed Cador Bane — the *Honourable* Cador Bane, if you please.

It was hard to believe they were brothers. In almost every respect, Cador was Talan's complete opposite. Where Talan was tall and spare, Cador was short and stocky. Where Talan was pale, Cador had a ruddy, raddled complexion that betrayed his fondness for the bottle. Where Talan exuded elegance and refinement, Cador looked more like a common footpad, with his once-broken nose, cool blue eyes and pitted jaw.

Neither did Cador possess his brother's grasp of the social graces. He had merely glared at her for a moment before grunting a perfunctory greeting, and had appeared even less enthusiastic when they finally arrived at the inn, where Talan said he had business with the owner, Abel Keskey . . . for it was here that Talan suddenly declared that so fine a lady could not possibly be expected to lodge in such humble surroundings.

'You must stay at Bane House for the remainder of your visit to Penderow,' he decided, as if the idea had just occurred to him. 'I will brook no refusal, my dear lady.'

There was, of course, little chance of that. Elizabeth had known from the start that they were merely playing a game, something akin to a courtship ritual, wherein he would seek to win her over so that he might bed her.

Again, she was under no illusions. This wasn't about love, though perhaps one day it could be. Rather, it was about lust — his for her, and her own long-held need to climb above her station. Consequently, each of them saw the other as but a means to an end, and she had no problem at all with that. Indeed, introducing *love* into the matter would only complicate it, and she felt that he had no more desire to complicate their relationship than did she.

In any case, he was attractive, and she suspected that he would be a good and attentive bed-partner. He might also prove to be more generous than Benjamin had ever been . . . and so, for the moment, she was content.

Initially, however, her introduction to Bane House had been a disappointment. Once, it had been unquestionably magnificent. Now it was but a run-down shell of its former self, with tall but crooked chimneys projecting from a steeply-pitched roof that was badly in need of patching, and dead vegetation clinging limply to its crumbling red-brick walls.

As if sensing her disapproval, Talan had hurriedly explained that their father had squandered much of the family's wealth before he died, and that he and his brother were now trying to restore the place, and planning to introduce to its twenty-six rooms the almost unheard-of luxury of gas lighting.

She sensed that he was lying about his father, but the rest was borne out by the fact that part of the mansion was covered in wooden scaffolding and ladders, and a handful of local labourers were carrying out renovation work with varying degrees of enthusiasm.

She suspected that the room she had been given was among the best, especially after seeing the poor state of the lobby. Good — that meant Talan was serious about trying to impress her.

The only real problems, she concluded, were Talan's brother and their surly manservant, Yestin Treffale.

Cador had remained silent throughout much of the morning, his silence laced heavily with disapproval. She had overlooked this because she wanted to avoid anything that might make Talan question the wisdom of his invitation. But perhaps, after she had curried sufficient favour with him, she would comment upon Cador's attitude and get Talan to do what he could to change it. She might even attempt to win Cador over herself, to further establish her place here.

The brothers' manservant, too, was a gruff, impolite sort. He was a tall man with heavy, ugly features and waxy skin. When Talan had introduced him, it had seemed to her that Treffale resented her every bit as much as Cador had. And yet he was merely a servant. What right did he have to question the actions of his master?

But that was something else curious about Treffale. At no time did he ever *behave* like a servant. There was neither deference nor respect in him — he treated Talan and Cador as casually as if he were their equals, and at no time did either of the brothers ever pick him up upon it.

Once again she looked around the room, with its fine, veneered or inlaid furniture. There was a wardrobe, a toilet table, chairs, a modest display of books and a wash-stand beside a tall mirror. She wanted for nothing.

If she gave Talan what she knew he wanted, if she used every one of her womanly wiles, she would eventually convince him that he could never do without her. And when that day came she would become the mistress of Bane House.

It was a title that made her skin tingle pleasantly.

And once she was mistress, she promised herself that Treffale would learn the true meaning of deference.

They *all* would.

★　★　★

Downstairs in the sitting room, Cador threw back another glass of brandy, the movement so quick with anger that he spilled most of the liquid down his pitted chin and irritably sleeved it away. Talan watched him stumble unsteadily back to the decanter and pour himself a refill.

'Go easy with that,' Talan advised. 'Until we get some more money, we've got to make it last.'

Cador spun on him. '*Money!*' he hissed. 'Do you know something, dear

146

brother? I am *sick* of having to watch every farthing! I have come to *despise* it! I never want to worry about money ever again!'

'You can despise it no more than I,' Talan assured him.

'And yet you have introduced a new and needless expense into our lives.'

Ah, thought Talan. There it was, then — the real reason for Cador's foul humour. 'You refer, of course, to the woman.'

Cador staggered back to his chair and slumped into it. 'I cannot for the life of me see why you invited her here in the first place! Especially if Abel Keskey's right, and we have another of our little . . . *enterprises* . . . coming up.'

'I invited her here because I am a man and I have *needs*, brother,' Talan said tightly. 'And that woman is clearly available.'

'But she's an *outsider*,' Cador protested. 'One who may well see too much and then put two and two together unless we play things close to our chests!'

'Then that is what we shall do.'

Cador shook his head, the movement loose and ill-controlled. 'I can't believe you would risk this entire enterprise upon a whim.'

Talan studied him for a long, curious moment. Finally he said, 'Are you at all familiar with the word 'mercenary', dear brother?'

'Eh?'

'It derives from the Latin word *mercénnàrius*, which in turn comes from the word *mercés*, meaning wages.'

'How fascinating,' Cador slurred sarcastically.

'The charming Mrs Masterson is as mercenary as you or I, Cador — meaning that she has only her own interests at heart, and to the devil with such trifles as honour and ethics. She craves everything and will *give* everything to satisfy that craving. With you and I she sees an opportunity that is too good to ignore. Do you see what I'm driving at?'

'Not especially.'

'Even if she *does* find out about the way we make our money, do you think she will give a tinker's cuss? Of course not, brother! She is as venal as you and I. And she will happily give of herself for reward — '

' — just like a common whore,' said Cador.

'Of course,' said Talan. 'But there is the beauty of it, Cador, for she *is* no common whore. Indeed, I fancy that she will prove to be rather *un*common between the sheets, a woman of some refinement whose grunts and thrusts will have a little more sincerity to them than those of a common trollop.'

Thinking about the woman and the promise he saw in her, he went across to the door, intending to make sure she was properly settled in . . . and properly grateful for the kindness he had shown her.

'The woman presents no danger to us,' he assured Cador. 'Indeed, she may well prove to be an ally. Besides . . . '

He allowed the sentence to trail off.
'What?' asked Cador.

Talan smiled coolly. 'You can have her when I am done with her,' he said callously. 'And then Yestin, if he is of a mind.'

13

Ennor Deveral might have been many things, but blind wasn't one of them. And the change in Meg, when she came back from the Point that day, was plain to see.

Something had upset the girl. Was it Ellen? Had she taken a turn for the worse? He asked and Meg told him no. Elizabeth, then — Jack's wife; was she still there, making trouble as they'd expected? No.

'Then what *is* it, *douter?*' he asked. '*Something's* upset you.'

But Meg only shook her head. 'It's nothin', Da. I'm tired, that's all. After all, none of us got much sleep last night, did we?'

He didn't press her on the matter, but knew beyond any doubt that something had happened to upset her. And if it wasn't anything to do with

Ellen and it wasn't anything to do with Elizabeth . . . that only left Jack.

Had *he* done something to upset her? Ennor could hardly imagine it. The man was just too straight. He'd never do anything to hurt anyone else . . . at least not intentionally.

Unable to solve the mystery, he told himself to mind his own business. He'd wait and see how Meg was on the morrow.

But 'quiet and subdued' was how she was. She went about her chores with her usual diligence, but there was nothing bright about her, and he'd grown used to that brightness ever since Jack and Ellen had come into their lives.

Around the middle of that morning Ennor asked when Meg was planning to walk up to the Point and check on Ellen. Her response was a restless shrug. 'Why don't *you* go up there today, Da?' she suggested. 'Ellen will be pleased to see you, and the walk'll do you good.'

Again he chose not to make anything of it. 'Aye,' he agreed placidly, and went outside to get his jacket. 'Happen you're right.'

The day was overcast and the wind had a definite chill to it. Ennor shuffled steadily through the village with his hands shoved deep into his pockets and his head down, partly to shield his face from the bitter wind and partly to avoid the still-accusing glares of all those former friends who now believed completely that he had thrown in with the wreckers . . . whoever they were.

When he reached the Point, Jack looked both surprised and disappointed to see him. Clearly he'd been hoping to find Meg at the front door instead. He invited Ennor inside, and Ennor was delighted to see Ellen seated at the table, some paper and a scattering of coloured beeswax crayons set out before her.

'Hello, little princess!' said Ennor. 'I didn't expect to see you up and about so soon!'

Jack muttered, 'It was either let her get up or risk a mutiny.'

Ennor went and gave the girl a gentle hug. Ellen still looked pale but was obviously on the mend. 'I'm drawing a picture,' she said.

'Aye, so I see. And a very pretty picture it looks, too.' He cocked his head and gave an exaggerated frown as he studied the illustration. 'It seems to me I *know* that face.' And then: 'Why, bless me — it's your doll, isn't it? Polly!'

Ellen clapped her hands together, pleased that he'd recognized the subject. 'Where's Meg?' she asked.

His face clouded. 'Ah, she's . . . busy today, lass, but she sends her love. How are you feeling now, anyway?'

'A bit sore,' said Ellen. 'But it's not too bad so long as I take my time moving about.'

'Well, you'll heal fast now, my girl, and then we'll all have our work cut out just trying to keep up with you!'

She giggled.

'Can I get you a cuppa, Ennor?' asked Jack.

Ennor nodded. 'Aye, why not?'

He followed the younger man across to the sink and lowered his voice. 'What's going on, lad?'

'Going on?'

'You look about as cheerful as my Meg — which isn't very cheerful at all, right now. Have you two had a falling out, or something?'

Jack was about to shake his head, then changed his mind. Ennor was nobody's fool, and would see right through any attempt he made to lie.

'A falling-out might have made things simpler,' he said. 'What has Meg told you?'

'Nothing. But her face says it all. She came up here all merry and bright and when she came home again she looked just the way she did the day her dear mother passed away.'

Jack dropped his head and sighed. 'I never wanted to hurt her, Ennor.'

'I believe you, lad. If I didn't I'd have

155

knocked your block off by now. But whatever happened between you *did* hurt her. Hurt you as well, if your expression's anything to go by.'

'It did. But . . . ' Jack hesitated a moment, then said, 'Did Meg tell you about the, ah, visitor I had yesterday morning?'

Keeping his own voice pitched low so that Ellen wouldn't hear, Ennor said, 'Your wife? Aye. I saw her arrive and asked Meg who she was.'

'Did she tell you that Elizabeth had walked out on us?'

'She did.'

'Well, here's the way it is. I've grown fond of your Meg, Ennor — more that fond, if truth be told. And as it turns out, she says she feels the same way about me, and though she's young and knows little of the world, I believe her. But I'm a married man — something I chose to forget until Elizabeth walked back into my life — and there's no way the likes of me can *unmarry*.

'If I can't court your daughter the

way she deserves to be courted, if I can't put a ring on her finger and make an honest woman of her, then there's only one thing I can do — I have to step aside and make way for a man who can.'

Ennor nodded sadly. 'Well said, lad. But she doesn't see it that way?'

'I think she does, deep down. She just doesn't *want* to.'

'Then all you can do is give it time,' Ennor decided. 'She might not like it, but sooner or later she'll see the truth of it and then, no matter how hard she finds it, she'll have to accept it.'

'I hope so, Ennor,' Jack said with feeling. 'I hope the *both* of us can.

* * *

Elizabeth Masterman, now calling herself Elizabeth Master*son*, wasted no time in making her presence felt at Bane House.

Late that first evening Talan knocked softly at her bedroom door and when she told him to enter, he pretended that he had come simply to make sure that everything was to her liking and that she was happy with her quarters.

Elizabeth had looked him straight in the eye, knowing that this predatory man would like her boldness, the fact that she was as aware as he of the truth of their situation and that there was no need for further play-acting.

'I am more than happy,' she replied huskily, coming closer to him. 'You have been my saviour, Talan, and I am *more* than grateful.'

She had reached for him then, the movement so brazen and, for him, so unexpected, that his eyes had widened in surprise and he had gasped softly.

After that everything had become a kaleidoscope of sounds and images. He had grabbed her and dragged her urgently toward him; their mouths had crushed together; and then he had walked her backwards to the bed and she had gone willingly, knowing that this was her opportunity to accede to his every demand and in the process ensure that he could not live without her.

She fell onto her back and he in turn fell upon her, crushing her with his weight. She had heard his fractured breathing in her left ear, his whispered compliments and promises of pleasure to come and she had replied in kind.

The soft sliding of cloth from skin as each undressed the other, the feel of his hands exploring her, the sexual heat that belched from him, the giddy taste and smell of passion —

He did not last long, that first time, but after he was spent she whispered comforts and compliments about his abilities. She had no idea if he believed her or not. He wanted to, and she was a very good liar.

The second time he showed more restraint and control, and as she stared up at the canopied ceiling of the four-poster she told herself that she had been right — he *was* an attentive lover.

She responded with an enthusiasm

and abandon she was sure he had never known before. His excitement told her she was right. And by the end of the evening, when finally he withdrew from her room and left her to doze contentedly, she knew he was hers to command.

And command she did, over the next several days.

When she wasn't trying to win Cador over at mealtimes — more or less the only times she ever got to see him — she was passing along 'suggestions' to Treffale.

At the end of supper one evening, for example, she *suggested*, 'The next time you roast beef, Treffale, you should add some chopped onions, carrots and perhaps even a stick of celery to the joint. Add leak and garlic for good measure, but leave the skin on the garlic, for it is not for eating, merely for flavor. Oh, and wash it first.'

Treffale only bit his tongue and nodded.

Whilst walking with Talan in the

garden one afternoon, she *suggested* that he should consider establishing an arboretum in the grounds. 'It will beautify your surroundings,' she said, knowing better than to refer to them as *our* surroundings just yet.

'They are still enormously fashionable,' she continued gaily, 'and their picturesque appearance can bring to mind all the climes from whence they came.'

'Can they, indeed?' he asked, smiling.

'Oh yes. The right choice of trees can conjure the snowy wastes of the Himalaya, the steaming savannahs of the wide Missouri, the valleys of Lebanon and the unexplored forests of darkest Patagonia.'

He laughed and she looked up at him, her temper flaring. But to her surprise he was looking at her with an expression she had never truly expected to see — genuine appreciation.

He actually seemed to be developing *feelings* for her.

During the days she was his almost

constant companion. At night she was his unashamed whore. Slowly, carefully, she began to insinuate herself into his life more and more. When she *suggested* that he allow her to oversee the daily running of the house, he argued that there was little enough to run, and that Treffale could manage admirably.

'But it will not always be so,' she reminded him. 'As your dream to restore Bane House comes to fruition, so you will rise through the ranks of your rich and esteemed neighbours. They will call upon you, Talan, for all manner of things — your friendship, your advice, your patronage, or simply to invite you into their own circles — and when that day comes you will need to rest assured that your home is being run efficiently and well.'

He considered that. 'But there is no money for staff,' he argued. 'At least, not yet.'

'But there *will* be,' she returned. 'You are a remarkable man, Talan, perhaps more remarkable than you know. You have already accomplished so much.'

He had, of course, done no such thing. He had, she felt, wasted his life and squandered his many wonderful opportunities. But with the right woman behind him, to push and guide and inspire him . . .

At length he nodded. 'You're right, Elizabeth,' he said, realising perhaps for the first time what really lay ahead for him — the potential for respectability. 'When Bane House is restored, we will have certain . . . responsibilities.' And squeezing her hand, he added, 'I will very seriously consider your suggestion.'

14

Of course, Elizabeth knew she still had much to do before Talan was completely in her thrall. For one thing, he still kept far too many secrets from her, and that meant he had yet to trust her completely. Although he seemed happy to spend most evenings in her company, however, on this particular night he requested that she remain in her room alone, for he was expecting what he called 'a personal visitor'.

At first she suspected that it was another woman. She had come to learn that Talan was a man of considerable appetites; appetites that even she could never hope to satisfy all by herself. Thus, she was willing — albeit reluctantly — to allow him his concubines . . . as long as he exercised discretion and understood that she and she alone was the *true* mistress of Bane House.

Late on in the evening there came a hollow, businesslike rapping at the front door. Hearing it echo up through the house, Elizabeth immediately left her room and tiptoed to the shadowy head of the stairs, eager to get a glimpse of her competition. But when Treffale opened the door, she saw to her surprise that the visitor was Abel Keskey, the innkeeper.

What the devil was *he* doing here?

Keskey and Treffale exchanged a few words. They spoke quietly — in the manner of conspirators, she thought — and unfortunately she was unable to hear their conversation. Then Treffale closed the door and accompanied Keskey across the lobby and into the sitting room. The double doors closed behind them and the gloomy, ill-lit lobby fell silent.

Unable to resist her curiosity, Elizabeth cautiously descended the staircase, determined to listen in on the meeting that followed, and discover for herself what it was that Talan wished to keep so secret from her.

It was a decision she was to regret.

* * *

'What is the news?' asked Talan, sitting forward eagerly.

And there *was* news, he was certain. Abel Keskey was perhaps the most important member of their small band. As an innkeeper he got to meet any number of folk and hear all the news, which made him an excellent source of information.

A portly fifty year-old with a round, jowly face and ruddy cheeks, Keskey took off his hat to reveal the wiry, steel-grey hair beneath, and scratched at his mutton-chop side-whiskers. ''Tis as I was led to believe,' he reported. 'There's a ship, a full-rigger known as the *McNair*, nineteen thousand tons fully-laden, coming from America and expected to pass this way tomorrow night. She'll be carrying silk and china, tools, shirts, vintage port and tobacco.'

166

Silence filled the room as the brothers and Treffale considered the announcement. 'We'll have to move quick,' Cador said at last. 'Tomorrow night . . . it doesn't give us much time.'

'But it'll be worth it, I'm thinking,' Keskey added softly.

'Why?'

'Because that's not *all* she's carrying.' The innkeeper waited a moment, then said, 'She's transporting a cargo of cannel coal, too.'

Greed suddenly flared in his audience.

Cannel coal was, as its name implied, a type of coal. It burned easily and brightly, and left little ash. But its true worth lay not so much in its use as a fuel as in its gaseous content. Cannel coal contained an excess of hydrogen, which was even now being extracted for use by the evergrowing gas manufacturing industry, and demand was high.

Put simply, it would fetch a high price indeed . . . *if* they could wreck the *McNair* and successfully seize her cargo.

'We've got to chance it,' said Treffale.

Talan nodded. 'Aye. If we handle this well, it'll set us up handsomely for a good, long while.'

'We'll need men,' decided Cador. 'Ten, at least.'

'I can get 'em,' said Keskey.

'So what's the plan?' asked Treffale.

'The usual,' Talan decided. 'We douse the light at Penderow Point and wait for the *McNair* to break up on the Devil's Teeth below. While she's foundering, we board her, subdue her crew and then unload her.'

No man there had to ask what Talan meant by *subdue*.

He meant *kill*.

'We'll need a good few wagons to transport the plunder,' said Treffale, thinking ahead.

Cador disagreed. 'Not necessarily. It's only a short journey to the mine.'

He was referring to Wheal Hazel, an abandoned copper mine six or seven miles up the coast from Penderow Point, which had been named for their mother. Before the decline in demand for copper had led to its closure, it had been a profitable business for the Bane family, its narrow shaft reaching deep into the bowels of the earth before turning sharply to the south, where it bored into the stuffy darkness far below the churning Celtic Sea.

'We can run two or three wagons back and forth until we're done,' he continued. 'Then, once everything's hidden away, we'll wait for a month or so, as usual, and then start moving everything out again in smaller shipments, as and when we sell it.'

'I'll arrange for the men and wagons, then,' said Keskey. 'But what about the light?'

'What about it?'

'The new man, Masterman,' Keskey went on. 'He's younger than Ennor Deveral, and like as not sharper. And since he's already heard how we duped Deveral the night we wrecked the *Persephone*, we can't try *that* trick again.'

'We're not going to,' Talan replied

almost immediately. 'We're going to kill him and be done with it.'

Silence poured into the room.

'We'll make it look like an accident,' Talan assured them all quickly. 'We'll catch him in the lantern room and make it look as if he slipped, fell down the stairs and broke his neck.'

'But . . . but why?' asked the innkeeper.

'Because he's a *threat*, Abel, and we'll all be safer without him nosing around.'

'I'm not so sure about that,' said Treffale. 'I've been keeping an eye on Masterman ever since Ned Magowan told us he'd been asking questions down at the Peacock, and watching Deveral's daughter, too, ever since Magowan went to see her the very next day. Neither one strikes me as being a threat, leastways not anymore.'

'But what about *after* the event?' countered Talan. 'Suppose we take Masterman by surprise, knock him senseless and tie him up until it's all over. What happens *then?* He was quick enough to take Ennor Deveral's side when he first got here. He certainly won't rest until he's proved his *own* innocence.'

'He'll never manage that.'

'Perhaps not. But if he makes enough noise about it, Trinity House might decide to reopen the case against Deveral. Then we're all in danger.'

Cador considered that for a moment, then nodded. 'I think you're right, brother. It's best he dies.'

'But he's got a *child,*' objected Keskey. 'A little girl.'

'That's not our concern,' said Talan dismissively. 'She'll be all right. Someone will take her in.'

Treffale nodded. 'All right, Talan,' he said. 'I don't like it, but I can see the sense to it.'

'Then — '

But Talan bit off whatever he was about to say next, and instead quickly turned toward the closed doors, beyond which he thought he had heard the tell-tale creak of a floorboard. Without another word he hurried across the room, tore open the doors, went out into the darkened lobby — and saw nothing.

For a moment then he had thought —

But before he could heave a sigh of relief, he caught the faintest sound and twisted toward the staircase.

Elizabeth was standing about halfway up, pressing her back against the wall, hoping vainly he wouldn't see her in the semi-darkness.

He looked up at her, into what he could see of her shadowed face, and her expression told him everything he needed to know. She had been listening at the door, heard everything they'd said; and having heard it, had tried to creep back to her quarters, there to . . . to *what*?

'Elizabeth,' he said, forcing himself to keep his voice soft and reasonable.

She made no reply.

Feeling his anger building, Talan said, 'Elizabeth, come down here.'

She made no move.

He went slowly toward the foot of the staircase, his heavy, ponderous steps the only sound in the otherwise silent house, and then he began to climb unhurriedly, so as not to frighten her.

'Elizabeth,' he said, his voice still low, placating. 'Whatever you think you heard just now . . . '

'I . . . I didn't hear anything,' she said quickly.

'I'm glad you heard it,' he continued, as if she hadn't spoken. 'Yes, *glad*. Because if you're to stay here and look after the house, if you're to look after *me* . . . then there should be no secrets between us.'

When no more than four steps separated them, she said, 'Stay back, Talan.' Her voice was choked, scared.

'Elizabeth — '

'*Stay back, I said!*'

Her cry echoed up toward the roof, sounding hollow and fraught.

'We have to talk about this,' he told her.

'What — about the fact that you are little better than a common thief?' she returned. 'And worse — that you talk of murdering Jack and — '

Without warning he froze.

'*Jack?*'

'The . . . the light-keeper,' she hedged. 'I . . . I heard you mention his name.'

'Perhaps you did,' he allowed. 'But you didn't hear me mention his *first* name.'

The silence was now complete, and so full of menace that she felt compelled to break it.

'You . . . you can't *murder* him, Talan,' she implored. '*Please*. I will overlook anything, *anything*, but you must promise me not to do that!'

He cocked his head at her. 'Who is he to you, this man?'

'He is nothing to me,' she replied honestly. 'It is for the girl that I ask.'

He climbed one more step, something unpleasant beginning to stir within him. 'Who *are* you, Elizabeth?' he asked. 'Who are you, really?'

She made no reply. But by then she didn't need to. He had worked it out for himself, and the knowledge made him feel vaguely sick. The lighthouse keeper's name was Masterman. She had said her name was Master*son*. The names were too similar for coincidence. And now that he thought about it, they had first picked her up just a short way from Penderow Point.

'Is he your husband?' he demanded.

'*Please* . . . ' she whispered, and began to cry.

'Is he?' he asked. And when no answer was forthcoming: '*Is he?*'

His voice echoed around the darkened lobby.

Her reply was wrenched from her. 'Yes! Yes, he is! But we are estranged, and have been for months! He means nothing to me, Talan, I swear it, and after all the arguments we've had I suspect I mean even less to him! But he . . . he is a good man, and more than that he is a good father! My daughter would be cast adrift without him,

175

and — ' emotion choked her suddenly, ' — and by my own actions alone she has already suffered heartbreak enough!'

She might have said more, but just then her eyes shuttled from his unreadable face to a spot behind him, as first Cador, then Treffale, then Keskey, came to stand in the sitting room doorway.

Her nerve broke completely then, and she turned and started back up the stairs as fast as she could go. If she could just lock herself in her bedroom, if she could find something with which to protect herself, if she could then find some way to escape and forewarn Jack —

Fingers suddenly gripped her arm and yanked her around.

She screamed.

Talan grabbed her by both arms, shook her, then slapped her. She stumbled backwards, almost fell, then lashed out, raked his face with her nails. He roared, reached for his burning cheek, and she continued up the staircase, up, up —

He raced after her, temper not just flaring now but exploding, four thin streaks of blood beading on his skin and coursing down his cheek as he went.

At the head of the stairs he once more caught her by the arm and shook her much as a terrier shakes a rat. His face was wild, eyes large, teeth clenched.

Again she screamed, struggled against him, but he was really *furious* now; furious that she was not entirely the conscienceless woman he had thought her to be, the woman with whom he had stupidly almost convinced himself he was falling in love, the woman who would sooner betray him to the authorities than stand beside him and enjoy the wealth he promised to attain.

She fell backwards, collided with a small ornamental table, and he went down with her. He heard the heavy thump her head made striking the floor and snarled, 'What am I supposed to do with you now, eh? What am I supposed to do?'

She made no answer.

Still angry, he dug his fingers into her bare shoulders and shook her some more. 'I can't let you go! I can't trust you not to betray me! So what am I supposed to — '

But then his voice dried up as, finally, he realised just how limp she felt in his arms, and he let go of her, allowing her to fall back to the floor. She was unconscious, unable to hear him.

Then he saw the blood.

It was pooling beneath her head, where she had struck the floor, and seized by a sudden panic, he snatched her up again, shook her this time in the hopes of reviving her.

She remained slack, her eyes closed, her head flopping loosely on the pale column of her neck.

Sensing from Talan's sudden silence that something bad had happened, the others hurried upstairs. Talan, meanwhile, pulled Elizabeth forward and inspected the back of her head. He made a curious moaning sound. Her hair was matted and bloody.

'What have you done?'

It was Treffale.

Talan looked around. 'I didn't do *anything!* She hit her head — '

Silence once again claimed then house, until Cador said, 'Is she . . . ?'

Talan could only shake his head. 'I don't know . . . '

Cador came forward, shoved his brother aside, peeled Elizabeth's eyelids back, then felt for her heartbeat, for a pulse at her wrist.

'She's dead,' he announced bluntly. 'She's dead, Talan — and you killed her.'

Talan's eyes went round. 'I didn't! You *know* I didn't!'

'Aye, but we're not the ones you'll have to convince,' said Treffale. 'A jury will decide that.'

Talan staggered upright, bewildered by this sudden turn of events and the very real possibility that he might yet keep an appointment with the gallows.

Think, man, think!

There had to be a way out of this,

there *had* to be . . .

And in the very next moment he found it.

He stared at his companions, and to their amazement, Talan's lips suddenly formed a cool smile.

'Listen to me,' he breathed. 'This is what we're going to do . . . '

15

When Meg came downstairs to make breakfast the following morning, she found her father already up and slumped in his favourite chair beside the hearth.

'Morning, Da'. You're up early.'

'Aye,' he said with a wince. 'Had the devil of a backache all night long. I think you might have been right, *douter* — I shouldn't have done all that digging in the garden.'

'You'll feel better after your breakfast,' she said, going through to the kitchen.

But after the meal he rose carefully from the table and, grabbing at the small of his back, said, 'It's no good, lass. Your poor old Da's showing his age at last.'

'Here,' she said, helping him back into the parlour, 'you just take it easy today.'

'I think I might have to,' he said, lowering himself carefully back into his chair. 'Shame — I was looking forward to going up to the Point and seeing young Ellen, too.' He took out his clay pipe and busied himself filling it with tobacco, adding casually, 'Looks like you'll have to go instead.'

She immediately shook her head, the prospect of seeing Jack again almost too painful to even contemplate. 'Oh, I . . . I've got too much to do here, Da'.'

'But I promised her,' he replied. 'I can't let her down. She'll be expectin' me.'

'Maybe later,' she said.

'Oh, leave it, then,' he said with uncharacteristic impatience, and struggled to get back up out of the chair. 'I'll go.'

She couldn't allow that — it was all he could do just to sit forward. 'Stay there,' she said, reaching for her shawl. 'I'll go.'

'Thank you, *douter*,' he replied, and with a tired sigh he sank back. 'Give that girl a hug for me.'

'I will.'

He waited until he heard the front

door close behind her, then sprang up out of the chair like a man half his age. He even managed to dance a little jig on his way into the kitchen to make a cup of tea.

He knew his daughter well. There was no way she'd ever go back to the Point and see Jack unless she was forced into it, and he considered that the small white lie he'd told about his poor old back was entirely justified if it helped to heal whatever breach had formed between them.

All the way up through the village and on toward Penderow Point, Meg struggled with conflicting emotions. On the one hand, she felt she would sooner go anywhere else, and see anyone other than Jack. But on the other she couldn't deny the excitement she felt at seeing him again.

Since the last time she'd seen him, she had given the situation endless hours of thought and knew he had only done what he considered was right. He hadn't made his decision to hurt her

— just the opposite. And for that reason alone she knew that she could not cut him out of her life forever. If they couldn't be together the way they wanted to be, then they would just have to be friends . . . though she had the feeling that would be harder, at least for her, than it sounded.

At last she reached the Point, went up to the cottage with wildly-beating heart and knocked at the door. When he answered the summons they both stood there for a moment, just looking at each other.

Meg swallowed softly. It was as difficult for her to see him again as she had expected it to be. He had come to mean so much to her, had come to dominate her thoughts so completely, that seeing him again even after such a relatively short interval was almost unreal.

He looked down at her, his expression a reflection of her own. At last he opened his mouth to say something, but before he could Ellen squeezed past him and almost threw herself at Meg in her haste to give their visitor an excited hug.

'I haven't seen you for ages!' said the child. 'Dad told me all about how you helped me that night when I was ill.'

Meg hugged her back. 'Well, we all did what we could,' she replied. She held the girl at arm's length so that she could examine her. 'You certainly *look* well. How do you feel?'

'A lot better,' Ellen replied with a nod. 'I'm going back to school tomorrow.' She pulled a face, but almost immediately brightened again. 'Come and see all my drawings!'

Taking her by the hand, Ellen more or less dragged her into the cottage and through to her bedroom, where all the drawings she'd done during her convalescence were piled neatly on her little chest of drawers. Jack closed the cottage door and followed them as far as the bedroom. There he leaned against the doorframe, watching as Ellen asked Meg if she would like to hear some of the stories she'd written, and Meg said she would love to.

For a moment his rugged face clouded and a dark mood threatened to overcome him. If only things could have been different . . .

But they weren't, and that was an end to it.

And yet as he stood there watching Meg, he couldn't help but feel again the injustice of it, that he had married once to the wrong woman and because of that was now forbidden to marry the right one.

Ellen led Meg across to the bed and they both sat side by side on the edge of the mattress. Ellen sorted through her little stack of drawings and writings until she found the page she was looking for. 'This is a story called *The Busy Little Bee*,' she said, and clearing her throat importantly, she began to read. ''Once upon a time . . . ''

Jack was distracted from the scene by another knock at the door, and thought that with two visitors in such quick succession he had never been so popular. But when he opened the door he found Constable Hendy standing outside, flanked by Yestin Treffale and Abel Keskey.

All three men were scowling.

'Good morning,' Jack said carefully. 'What can I — '

'If you please, sir, this is not a social call,' said the big-bellied policeman, squaring his shoulders. 'In fact, it's a call I never thought I'd make.'

Jack frowned. 'I'm sorry?'

'I am arrestin' you, sir,' Hendy said formally, 'for the murder of your estranged wife, Mrs Elizabeth Masterman.'

* * *

For one fleeting moment Jack thought he had misheard what the other man said. Elizabeth? Dead? *Murdered?* His stomach lurched unpleasantly and it seemed as if the world tilted drunkenly underfoot. There had to be some mistake —

Then Constable Hendy raised his

right hand, there was a cold rattle of metal against metal and Jack realised that he was holding a thick chain to which was attached two rusty shackles and a padlock. 'Hold your hands out, if you please, sir,' Hendy said grimly.

Instinctively Jack took a step away from him. 'You'll not shackle me,' he breathed. 'I haven't *done* anything!'

Having heard the exchange, Meg quickly stood up and told Ellen to stay where she was. Then Meg came out of the bedroom and closed the door behind her. 'What was that about Elizabeth?' she asked, her voice a little unsteady.

Ignoring her, Hendy said, 'Your hands, if you please, sir.'

Jack shook his head. 'The least you can do is tell me what I'm supposed to have done — and when.'

'Mr Keskey here is well aware of the ill-feeling between you and your wife,' Hendy said gravely. 'Upon her arrival in Penderow she took a room at the Peacock, and confided in him.'

'Confided what?' challenged Jack, his mind still racing.

'That you and she were separated,' said Keskey, speaking for the first time. 'That she left you because of your violent ways, then came back for the sake of your daughter.'

'*What?*'

'Only to have you threaten her again,' Keskey continued, playing his part to the hilt. 'That poor woman was beside herself with fear. Fear for her daughter and fear for her own safety, after you threatened her.'

'*Threatened* her? I didn't even know she was still in Penderow!'

'Well, I know that you threatened to kill her if she ever came near you again,' Keskey said remorselessly. 'And when she failed to return from a walk yesterday afternoon, I started to fret for her.'

Hendy, believing the story completely, gave an emphatic nod. 'And it appears he had good cause. Abel was just about to go in search of her when

189

Mr Treffale here turned up to say that he had found her dead, *beaten* to death, and hidden in the woods.'

Jack shook his head dazedly. The shock was such that he was still having difficulty keeping it all straight in his mind. 'I didn't do it.'

'Can you prove that?' countered Hendy. 'Where were you yesterday afternoon and evening?'

'Here.'

'Do you have any witnesses?'

'My daughter,' said Jack, but immediately he shook his head again. 'No. She and Ennor went for a walk along the cliffs yesterday afternoon, they didn't get back until four.'

'The evening, then?'

'Ellen's been recovering from an operation. That and the walk tired her out and she went to bed early.'

'So you could have slipped out while she was a'bed, met your wife, perhaps having previously arranged to do so — and then killed her.'

'Aye, I could have,' Jack agreed

readily. 'But I *didn't*.'

'Well, your guilt isn't for me to decide,' said Hendy. 'It's a matter for the courts now.'

'You've no right to arrest him!' said Meg. 'You don't have a single scrap of evidence!'

'I have the testimony of Mr Keskey here, and that of Mr Treffale.'

'That means nothing!' protested Meg.

'I suspect a magistrate might see that differently,' said Hendy. 'Especially when he hears about Ned Magowan.'

Jack stiffened. 'Magowan? What the devil has *he* got to do with all this?'

'Only that *you* discovered the body,' said Hendy. 'And that he had suffered a head injury not unlike that we found on your late wife.'

'Funny, that,' murmured Treffale.

Again Hendy held out the manacles. 'Are you coming peaceably or what?'

'I'll come,' said Jack. 'But you've no need for those chains. I'm innocent, and with any luck good sense will prevail when this thing comes to trial.'

Meg blanched. '*Jack!*'

Keeping his eyes on Hendy, Jack said, 'Just let me say goodbye to my daughter first.'

It was on the tip of Hendy's tongue to refuse the request, but when it came to it he couldn't say no. 'Make it quick,' he said gruffly.

Jack turned and looked at Meg. Tears shone in her eyes. He opened his mouth, wanting to say . . . *something*. But no words would come. Dejectedly then, he went into his daughter's room and softly closed the door behind him.

'He *is* innocent,' said Meg. 'Anyone can tell that just by looking at him!'

Hendy eyed her with clear disapproval. 'For all I know, you were in it *with* him.'

'*What?* How dare — '

'You can't deny that you, your father and the light-keeper there have been as thick as thieves ever since he arrived.'

Blinking the tears from her eyes, Meg drew herself up. 'When Jack proves his innocence and the real murderer is brought to account,' she said, low-voiced, 'I will expect an apology from you, constable.'

Her gaze was so fiery, so direct, that as much as he tried not to, Hendy visibly squirmed until Treffale came to his rescue. 'He's taking his time, isn't he?' he muttered, jerking his overlarge chin toward the bedroom door.

Hendy caught the implication at once, and rudely shoved past Meg and then more or less tore the door open.

Ellen was sitting on the edge of the bed, looking scared.

Of Jack there was no sign.

Hendy's eyes travelled at once to the half-open window. He ran to it, saw nothing but the storage shed and, beyond it, the rugged, open coastline. Then he turned and stormed back outside.

'He's gone!' he announced for the benefit of his two companions. 'The scoundrel's made a run for it!' He hauled up sharp and turned on Meg.

'Still think he's innocent, do you?'

Without waiting for a reply, he left at a breathless run with Treffale and Keskey at his heels.

16

As Meg closed the door behind them Ellen asked softly, 'Meg . . . where did my Dad go?'

Meg turned to the little girl, who had come out of her bedroom and was staring up at her with trembling lips. Not knowing what else to do, Meg knelt and hugged her. 'There's been some trouble . . . ' she said.

'To do with my Mum?' asked the child. 'I heard that policeman say her name.'

Meg's throat tightened. How did she tell the child such terrible news? She squeezed Ellen's shoulders. 'Yes, she . . . she had an accident and . . . and she had to go to Heaven.'

Ellen considered that. She didn't really know how to react. It had been such a long time since she had seen her mother that she was little more than a memory now.

'What kind of accident?' she asked at length.

'A fall,' Meg said vaguely.

'Why were those men shouting at my Dad?'

'They weren't shouting,' said Meg. 'But they . . . they thought he might be able to help them . . . explain exactly what had happened to her.'

'Why did he climb out of my window and run away?'

That, Meg decided, was a very good question. She didn't think for one moment that Jack had deserted his daughter in order to save his own skin. And she didn't believe he had done what Constable Hendy had accused him of. But at the back of her mind she could hear his voice, the day he had told her there could be no future for them.

I have no feelings for that woman one way or the other. But seeing her again reminded me that in the eyes of the law I'm still married, and as long as Elizabeth lives, I can never give you the commitment you deserve.

As long as Elizabeth lives . . .

Abruptly Meg rose to her feet. The very idea that Jack would resort to murder was unthinkable. As far as he was concerned, as far as they had *all* been concerned, Elizabeth had left the village. And yet, according to Abel Keskey, she had stayed on, and he had become her confidante.

'Come on,' Meg decided. 'Let's pack some clothes for you. You'll stay with us until your Dad comes home again.'

'When will that be?' asked Ellen.

'Soon,' Meg said to reassure her.

But the truthful answer was that she just didn't know.

It could well be that they might never see Jack again.

* * *

When they arrived back at Olvey Row, Meg told her father the news while Ellen was upstairs, unpacking her things in Meg's room. Ennor paled visibly.

'That lad didn't kill his wife any more than the piskies did!' he said, naming the mischievous sprites who were said to live on the moorlands and other isolated parts of the county.

'Of course he didn't, Da,' she replied. 'But *someone* did.'

'Aye — and from what you tell me, it sounds like Abel Keskey was a bit too ready to point the finger at Jack.'

'You're not saying that Keskey — ?'

'No, *douter*. At least, I don't *think* I am. But it's odd, isn't it? A woman like Jack's wife, with all her airs and graces and ideas above her station, confiding in a man like Abel Keskey?'

Meg wrung her hands. 'Oh, Da', where do you suppose Jack's gone? And what do you think they'll do when they catch him?'

'Who says they *will* catch him?' Ennor replied. 'He's a canny lad. He'll lay low until the real culprit's brought to justice.'

'But what if the real culprit *isn't* brought to justice? What then?'

Ennor didn't even want to think about that, but as luck would have it a knock at the door saved him from having to word a response.

They stared at each other for a long, tense moment, each fearing the worst. Then: 'I'll get it,' said Ennor, and he got up and strode past her, all pretence of a bad back now forgotten.

Meg stood in the centre of the parlour, dreading the news, and when she heard the sound of men's' voices she convinced herself that someone had come to tell them that Jack had been captured.

She heard her father say brusquely, 'You'd better come in.'

He came back into the parlour with a small delegation of townsfolk behind him. There was tall, spare, spectacle-wearing Awen Visick, who was the nearest thing Penderow had to a head man, Constable Hendy, Dr Trewin, Abel Keskey and Yestin Treffale.

Ennor came to stand beside Meg and then faced their visitors. 'All right,' he said. 'You say you need to speak to me. Say your piece and then leave.'

'There's no call to be like that,' said Visick, uncomfortably.

Ennor, in no mood to suffer fools, raised his bushy eyebrows. 'No?'

'We need your help, Ennor,' said the head man.

'Oh, I *see*,' Ennor replied with heavy sarcasm. 'Well, that makes sense. You wouldn't have come near nor by if you didn't.'

'I take it young Meg here has told you what the new light-keeper did?'

'She told me what Hendy and his so-called witnesses *say* he did.'

'He escaped, Ennor. That's as good as an admission of guilt to me,' said Visick. 'But we're not here for that. Masterman's run off and that means the Point's been left untended.'

'And you want me to take his place, is that it?' Ennor shook his head, and when he spoke again his voice was laced with disgust. 'By the devil, you people've got some nerve.'

'I know we've had our differences — ' began Visick.

'*Differences!* You've more or less disowned Meg and me, and for why? Because you were as quick to judge us as you've been to judge Jack Masterman!' He glared at them all, his expression softening only when he came to Dr Trewin. 'I don't include you with the rest of these fair-weather friends, doctor. You've always given me the benefit of the doubt, and I appreciate that.'

'Well, we're in a bind, Ennor,' said Trewin. 'We've no one else to turn to.'

Ennor grimaced as he turned his attention back to Visick. 'I've half a mind to tell you what you can do with your request,' he said, 'but . . . all right; I'll tend the lighthouse till someone else can take over.'

'Thank yo — '

'Save your thanks, Visick,' said Ennor. 'I'm not doing it for you. I'm doing it for Jack, and all the brave men who ply these waters after dark.'

Hearing that, Meg stiffened suddenly as a new thought sprang into her mind. Treffale noticed her reaction and it made him study her with open curiosity. Perhaps he thought she might know where Jack had fled, but if he did, he didn't say anything.

Ennor gestured that their conversation was finished, and the townsmen filed back along the hallway to the front door. Treffale, the last to leave, looked at her a fraction longer than necessary, and her flesh crawled under his scrutiny.

At last Ennor closed the door behind them and as he shuffled wearily back into the parlour Ellen came downstairs to join them.

'Have they found my Dad?' she asked.

'Not yet, little princess, but he'll show up soon,' Ennor replied. Then he noticed Meg's expression and said, 'Would you, uh ... like to see some butterflies, child? Maybe you could draw them for me.'

Ellen thought about it. 'All right.'

He pointed toward the back door. 'Just outside the door on the left I've planted a little herb garden. Go and look at the little purple plants. That's thyme — and the butterflies love to fly around it.'

As the little girl let herself outside, Ennor squinted at Meg and said softly, 'What's wrong, *douter*?'

'Nothing,' she replied. 'But . . . '

'But what?'

'Well . . . I was just thinking about what you said just now, about the men who ply our waters after dark.'

'What about them?'

'We *know* Jack didn't kill his wife. But *somebody* did — and whoever it was is trying to frame Jack for the murder.'

'Aye — to save his own miserable neck.'

'Or to make sure Jack won't be there to tend the light tonight.'

He cocked his head inquisitively. 'Eh?'

'I'm probably wrong,' she said. 'But suppose there's another ship due tonight, or tomorrow night, and someone wants to make sure it gets wrecked?'

'It won't,' said Ennor. 'I'll see to that.'

'Well . . . you take care of yourself, Da'. You know, just in case. You lock yourself in that lantern room tonight and don't you open that door again for anyone.'

'If it'll set your mind at rest,' he said, 'I won't. I promise.'

Together Meg and Ellen made sandwiches to help see Ennor through the long night ahead. As they worked, Meg kept thinking about Jack. It could have been, as her father had said, that whoever had murdered Elizabeth had simply sought to shift the blame to her estranged husband. But what if there was more to it?

Abel Keskey and Yestin Treffale had seemed far too ready to blame Jack for the crime. But did it necessarily follow that they were the real killers? And if so, had they also killed Ned Magowan?

As far as she could see, Keskey was the only link between the two deaths. Elizabeth had lodged at his inn, Ned

Magowan had drunk there.

Ned Magowan . . .

She remembered how scared he had been, the day he showed up on her doorstep. He had been terrified for his life and as subsequent events had shown, he'd been right to be so.

I know how to keep my mouth shut, he'd said. *But they think I'll break. I know they do. That's why they're watchin' me. And they are, you know. They didn't think I'd notice, but I did. And that's what's forced my hand! If they think I'm goin' to talk, they'll do whatever it takes to stop me.*

The poor man . . .

But then, seemingly out of nowhere, she recalled something else he'd said during that brief encounter, and a tingle washed across her skin.

I wrote it all down. But I wasn't going to say anything. It was just for . . . you know, insurance.

It suddenly struck her that she might yet be able to prove her father's innocence — and if Abel Keskey had been involved at all with Ned's murder, or the wreckers, it might cast doubt on the man's claims about Jack and Elizabeth.

She decided to say nothing to her father. For one thing, she didn't want to build his hopes up. For another, he had enough to concern him right now, just looking after the lighthouse.

When he was fully provisioned Ennor shrugged into his jacket, reached for his cap and kissed both girls tenderly.

'Be careful, Da'.'

'I will, *douter*, don't you fret. And as for *you*, little princess, everything will work out. You'll see.'

After Ennor had left for the Point, Ellen said, 'What shall we do now? Shall we play a game?'

Meg looked down at her, so young, so trusting, so deserving of a better life than she'd had so far. 'We've got go somewhere first,' she replied. 'And find something very, very important.'

Ellen frowned. 'What?'

'A confession,' Meg said softly.

17

It didn't take long to reach Ned's tumbledown cottage in Tredray Lane. As they followed the thin, overgrown path down through the sad-looking avenue of skeletal trees, the place looked as forlorn as it had the day Meg and Jack had first gone there and discovered Ned's body.

The memory sent a shiver through Meg, reminding her — as if she needed reminding — that they were dealing with truly ruthless men.

As they followed the weed-strewn path to Ned's front door, Meg saw with relief that no one had thought to replace the lock, shattered when Jack had broken in after seeing Ned's body through the grimy parlour window. All she had to do was push and the front door swung open with an eerie creak.

Clutching her doll tightly to her

chest, Ellen examined the house warily. 'Would you prefer to wait out here?' asked Meg. 'With any luck I shouldn't be too long.'

'No, I'll come with you,' said Ellen. Then went inside.

The house was gloomy and silent. It smelled of damp, loneliness and neglect. In the tiny parlour — the same room in which Ned Magowan had been so cruelly murdered — Meg looked around and wondered where she should start her search.

She was looking for one or more sheets of paper, and because they were of great importance to Ned she felt he would have taken pains to hide them well. She checked every drawer in the old dresser, then dropped to her knees and peered into the dusty gloom beneath it, but found nothing.

She rummaged through all the clutter in the little cupboard behind the door, then checked the table drawers. When she was as certain as she could be that Ned's confession wasn't to be found in the parlour, she went back out into the passage and with her heart fluttering nervously, began to climb the rickety staircase.

She had climbed the first three steps before she realised that Ellen had made no move to follow her. She looked back and asked in a whisper, 'Are you all right?'

Ellen nodded, but she looked uneasy. 'I don't like it here.'

'All right. You just wait there for me. I'll be as quick as I can.'

Meg continued her ascent. Each step groaned softly beneath her, breaking the otherwise oppressive silence.

The cottage had two small, untidy bedrooms. Meg searched each one as quickly and thoroughly as she could. Still the confession eluded her. It came to her that perhaps Ned's killer had already found it and taken it. Ned might have confessed to having put everything down in writing before he was killed.

A wave of disappointment threatened

to overwhelm her.

She went back downstairs. Ellen was clearly relieved to see her. 'Can we go now?' she asked plaintively. 'I want to see if Dad's come home yet.'

Meg stroked her hair. 'Just let me have a quick look in the kitchen.'

This time Ellen accompanied her through the dismal, dirty house to the poky little kitchen at the back. As much as she wanted to rush, Meg forced herself to take her time and make sure she looked carefully in every conceivable place.

At the end of her search, however, she was no closer to finding the vital paperwork, and was just about to concede defeat when she realised she hadn't yet checked the small larder.

She went across and opened the door. The shelves were bare save for a few mouldy foodstuffs. She checked every shelf until she reached the bottom one. Then, and more by chance than anything else, she noticed that that one of the thin wooden slats that formed the back of the larder seemed to be very slightly out of true with the rest.

When she touched it, the slat gave beneath her fingertips, as if at some time in the past it had been pried away from the rest and then replaced in such a way that only the shelves themselves held it in place.

As Ellen watched, Meg eased her fingertips around the edge of the slat, tugged it a little forward and to one side. With a dry scrape it moved to reveal a shallow gap between the back of the larder and the wall against which it had been built.

And there, in the gap, sat a single sheet of paper, folded twice, into a small oblong.

For a moment Meg just stared at it. Was this what she had been searching for? Had she actually found the evidence she needed?

She drew the sheet from its hiding-place and slowly, carefully unfolded it.

Her breath caught.

Ned Magowan's handwriting was

spidery at best, each line crowded tight to the one above and the one below. But it was unmistakably the confession he had mentioned.

My naem is Edward Magowan of number 1 Tredray Lane. If any one shuld find this dokument it is because some ill-fortune has befallen me and i have been silenced to keep me from telling what i know about a series of five wreckings that have taken place over the course of the last three years, 1839–1841 the last of which happened here in the villige of my berth, Penderow and involved the ship Persefonny. The people behind these acts in which i played my part are —

Meg jumped as the page was suddenly torn from her grasp, and she twisted around to find two men looming over her and Ellen, their faces twisted into masks of barely-controlled rage.

'I *told* you she was going to be trouble, didn't I?' whispered Yestin Treffale.

Beside him, Abel Keskey nodded grimly.

* * *

The day dragged for Ennor Deveral. Under any other circumstances he would have savoured every moment spent at his beloved Penderow Point, but today he felt more like a trespasser. Things had changed, and this place was no longer his, it belonged to Jack now. And poor Jack . . .

Time and again Ennor found himself wondering where Jack was hiding, what was going through his mind, whether or not he had been caught yet. Hadn't the poor man and his daughter already endured enough? Why did they have to suffer through something like this as well?

Stuck here at the point, Ennor felt helpless, absolutely unable to do anything to comfort Ellen, support Meg or help Jack; and that said a lot about just how Ennor's life had also changed in the past couple of weeks. Meg had always been the centre of his universe, especially after her poor mother had died. Now he realised how much Jack and Ellen had come to mean to him, too.

Low cloud began to roll in and turn the day overcast. It matched Ennor's mood. At about three o'clock he decided to go up to the lantern room and make sure everything was ready for the long night ahead — and that was when it happened.

He was about halfway between the lighthouse and the cottage when a voice off to his right and little behind him hissed, 'Deveral!'

Ennor stopped and turned around. A thick-set man he had never seen before had been skulking beside the cottage. Now he stepped forward, one hand hidden behind his back. Ennor, immediately on the alert, wondered who he was and what he was doing there.

'Do I know you?' he demanded.

The man shook his head. He had a

thick black beard and a dog-eared patch over his left eye, and he wore a threadbare Chesterfield coat over grey breeches tucked into well-scuffed boots. 'You don't *have* to know me,' he said, his raspy voice roughened by tobacco. 'But you'll do as I say, or your daughter will suffer a most unkind fate.'

Ennor tensed at the mention of Meg. 'What's that you've got to say about my daughter?'

'Simple,' said the other. 'If you want to see her again, her and the other one, the little girl, you'll make sure yonder light doesn't shine between eight and eleven tonight.'

Ennor's fists clenched. 'Wh . . . what have you done with Meg and Ellen?'

'Nothin',' said the one-eyed man. '*Yet*. And no harm will befall them, so long as you do as you're told.'

'You're a wrecker,' breathed Ennor.

'What I am is of no consequence to you,' the one-eyed man said harshly.

Temper flaring, Ennor took a step toward him. 'You'll tell me where they are and what you've done to them or — '

But the other man danced a quick step back, brought his hidden hand into view, and Ennor stopped dead in his tracks.

The man held Ellen's doll, Polly.

'We've got them, have no doubt on that score,' he said. 'And they'll be released, unharmed, when you've done as you've been told.'

Ennor swayed a little, the shock leaving him suddenly lightheaded. But when he looked at the man again, he actually jumped a little in surprise, and the man threw the doll to the ground at his feet and grinned. His teeth were big and yellow, and few and far between.

'Get it?' he asked.

'No,' said Ennor, shaking his head. 'But I've a very strong feeling that *you're* about to get it.'

Puzzled by the cryptic statement, the one-eyed man's grin disappeared and he said, 'What's that supposed to — ?'

The answer suddenly became all too

clear. A hand fell upon the man's shoulder, the fingers digging deep into the material of his Chesterfield and dragging him around. Startled, he suddenly came face to face with a newcomer whose arrival had been all but soundless.

Then —

The newcomer punched him hard on the jaw, and the one-eyed man went down on legs like pudding.

'*Jack!*' hissed Ennor, hurrying over. 'Where the devil did you spring from?'

Jack was already dragging the one-eyed man back up into a sitting position, handling him none-too-gently in the process. 'I've been here all the time, man,' he replied. 'Never went further than the storage shed.'

'*What?*'

'I knew Hendy would think I'd made a run for it. It wouldn't even occur to him that I'd not go far. I decided it was probably the last place he'd ever think to look.'

'But . . . but, why, lad? Why run? Why

not let justice take its course?'

'Two reasons, Ennor. One — I've no faith in the kind of justice you'd find among these folk, not once they'd been stirred up; and two — I've been waiting for something like this to happen.'

Ennor looked baffled. 'You're talking in riddles, boy.'

Jack fixed him with a direct look. 'Elizabeth's death . . . that was something no one could have foreseen, and I don't mind admitting, it knocked me sideways. As for the rest of it . . . well, we always knew these wreckers were local men, didn't we? But proving it was next to impossible . . . unless I could somehow force their hand, flush them out into the open.

'So I wrote to a friend of mine at Trinity House — a friend who's as keen to catch these beggars as I am — and between us we contrived a plan to do just that.'

His grin was tight and harsh.

'A rumour found its way to the landlord of the Peacock,' he continued, 'the rumour of a ship that's due to sail past this very stretch of coastline tonight. It's called the *McNair* and it's loaded down with a tempting cargo indeed. There's just one thing the wreckers don't know. The ship doesn't exist outside of my imagination, Ennor. But the prospect of wrecking it has flushed them out, right enough.'

'So you didn't want to go far from the Point anyway . . . '

'No. I knew they'd have to come here sooner or later, if they wanted to douse the light. My hope was to catch them in the act, with this to give me an advantage,' — he drew a sturdy duelling pistol from his jacket pocket — 'and then deliver them to Constable Hendy.'

'It was a fine plan, lad, but it's gone wrong. You must have heard what this cove just said about Meg and Ellen.'

'Aye, I heard,' said Jack. 'But this fellow is going to tell us where we can find them, aren't you, One-Eye?'

At first the man only groaned blearily. Then Jack pressed the muzzle of the pistol against the bulbous tip of his fat nose, and after that the man's single eye focused quickly.

'I can't!' he breathed. 'My life won't be worth livin' if I do!'

'I've got some news for you, mister,' Ennor said, dropping to a crouch beside him. 'Your life won't be worth livin' if you *don't!*'

18

Ellen's tiny voice came softly through the quickly-fading darkness.

'Meg . . . I'm scared.'

Meg was scared, too, but she was determined not to let Ellen see it. They were sitting side by side on an upturned tea chest, and Meg was holding the little girl close. 'It's all right,' she said, trying to hide the unease in her own voice. 'Everything's going to be all right.'

But she really didn't see how.

After Yestin Treffale and Abel Keskey had surprised them in Ned Megowan's kitchen, a brief, muttered conversation had ensued between the two men. Although Meg couldn't hear everything that was said, she got the impression that they didn't really know what to do with their prisoners now they'd captured them. But one thing was certain

— Meg now knew from Ned's confession that both men had been involved in the wrecking of the *Persephone* and others . . . knowledge that put both she and Ellen in a very precarious position.

Suddenly Keskey had nodded briskly at some muttered order from Treffale and left Ned's sorry-looking house in a hurry. A few moments later Meg finally found her voice.

'Wh . . . what is this all about, Mr Treffale? We . . . we haven't done anything wrong. We were only looking around.'

'Of course you were,' replied Treffale. His size and the strange, waxy pallor of his skin were frightening to the girls. 'But it's what you *found* while you were looking that's causing us such concern.' He raised the confession in his big right hand and waved it so that the paper made an angry snapping sound. 'And what you were going to *do* about it.'

Meg tried her best to appear puzzled. 'I don't know what you mean. We don't even know what that paper said. You snatched it away from me before I could read it.'

Treffale smiled, and his smile was perhaps the most frightening thing about him, for it was more of a cold peeling back of lips across teeth. 'You're not much of a hand at lying, are you?' he smirked.

'I wouldn't wish to be,' she replied defiantly.

Conversation died after that, and they all stood there, waiting, until at length there came the distinctive jingle and rattle of a wagon drawing up outside.

'We're all going for a little ride,' announced Treffale, gesturing that Meg and Ellen should precede him out of the kitchen. 'Behave yourselves and do as we say, and you won't be harmed. Do you understand me?'

Meg nodded. Ellen was too scared to do anything but stare fearfully up at the big, wax-faced man.

As soon as she stepped outside again Meg saw that Abel Keskey had fetched his delivery wagon, a modest-sized flatbed with a canvas canopy stretched over a series of four metal hoops. While Keskey kept lookout, Treffale herded the girls toward the back of the vehicle and then boosted each one into the wagon. He then climbed in behind them and tied the canopy tight while Keskey returned to the high seat and snapped a short whip over the rumps of his two-horse team to start them moving again.

There followed a slow and seemingly endless journey. With no way to see where they were being taken, Meg could only guess. After a while even that exercise became futile, for there was simply no knowing whenever they turned left or right.

At length the wagon rattled to a halt and the horses blew air through their flared nostrils. Treffale untied the canopy and hopped out, then gestured that the two girls should follow suit. Meg went first, then helped Ellen down.

They had arrived at a rugged, desolate spot overlooking the restless grey ocean. The deserted remains of several tumbledown wood- and brick-built structures stood around them, as did an enormous metal waterwheel, now red with rust, which still stood crookedly in its specially-designed pit. The place was empty of all save memories and, perhaps, the spirits of the men who had once toiled deep underground — aye, and under the very sea below — for the Bane family.

They had been brought to Wheal Hazel, the long-abandoned copper mine.

'Over there,' said Treffale, and he shoved Meg hard to get her moving.

Together she and Ellen walked toward the mine entrance, which at this late stage was little more than a vertical, grass-fringed shaft some six feet square, with a series of mouldy green rungs hammered into one wall to form a permanent means of access.

The rungs went straight down until they vanished into sheer, unbroken darkness.

'Down you go,' said Treffale.

Ellen clung to Meg, and Meg said, '*No!*'

'You either *climb* down or I *throw* you down, one at a time,' Treffale threatened gruffly.

'But — !'

'I'll be right behind you,' muttered Treffale.

That prospect offered no comfort.

Deciding that as long as they lived they had a chance to escape from this nightmare, Meg knelt and took Ellen's hands into her own. 'It'll be all right,' she said. 'Just follow me.'

Carefully Meg sat on the edge of the shaft and twisted herself around until she was holding onto the top-most rung. Then she began to descend, looking up all the while and forcing herself to smile encouragingly to Ellen.

Before Ellen could follow her down, however, Treffale snatched the little girl's doll from her and threw it to Keskey, who caught it awkwardly.

'That'll be a powerful persuader, I'm thinking,' he said. And then, to the little girl: 'Go.'

He began his own steady descent just

before Ellen disappeared completely into the darkness. Thereafter all Meg and Ellen could hear was their own nervous breathing, and the cold, metallic sounds they made descending ever deeper into the ground.

Treffale called over one shoulder, 'Have a care, Miz Deveral. The rungs will end shortly, but there'll be a ladder to take you the rest of the way down.'

Meg, already suffering from the close confines of the shaft, forced herself to keep going. A short while later she stopped abruptly, felt around in the darkness with one foot, searching for the next rung.

There wasn't one.

Carefully she lowered herself another few inches, until her foot touched the rung of a wooden ladder, which had been set at an angle against the wall.

She waited until Ellen was close enough to touch, then reached out with one hand to halt the girl. In the darkness she heard Ellen gasp.

'It's all right,' she said. 'Just be extra

careful now, because this is where the ladder takes over from the rungs in the wall.'

The ladder bowed a little beneath their weight as they climbed the last seven or eight feet. Without warning Meg reached the floor of the mine, then helped Ellen down the last few rungs to join her. A moment later they heard Treffale complete his own descent, and then winced at the sudden flare of light as he struck a white phosphorous match.

They were in a short tunnel with tight-packed earthen walls supported by thick props and cross-beams. Holding the match high, Treffale jerked his head to the left and said, 'Down there.'

They shuffled down the tunnel until it opened out into some kind of crude chamber that was filled with tea chests and other boxes of various sizes and shapes. Upon one of the boxes sat a stub of candle stuck by wax to a dusty saucer. Treffale lit the candle and the light chased some of the shadows aside.

'You'll be safe enough down here for the time being,' said Treffale, and without another word he turned back toward the exit.

'I don't like it!' wailed Ellen.

Meg took her hand and gave it a squeeze, watching as Treffale began to climb the ladder again. When he was out of sight, the sounds he made climbing suddenly stopped. Silence filled the abandoned mine, until Treffale grunted and then Meg saw to her horror that he had reached down to grab the ladder and was taking it up with him.

We're trapped, she thought. *Trapped with no possible means of escape.*

She grew aware then that the silence around them was actually anything *but* silent. It seemed to her that every pit-prop and cross-beam was groaning softly beneath the weight of thousands of tons of earth, and if she strained her ears especially hard, she could . . . yes, she *could* hear the restless wash of the sea, somewhere far above them!

'Meg?'

'I'm here, little princess.'

'I'm frightened.'

'Well, don't be. I'll protect you.'

She glanced at the stub of candle and wondered how much light they had left before the single, meagre flame finally guttered out in a pool of wax. It was bad enough down here now, as it was; in pitch darkness it would be so much worse.

They had to find some way of escaping from this makeshift prison.

'Come on,' she said, lifting the saucer and shielding the flame from any stray draughts. 'Let's have a look around. There might be another way out.'

There were a number of cobweb-festooned tunnels leading off from the main chamber, each one low of ceiling and barely four or five feet across. Meg felt her chest tighten at the very thought of going deeper into the mine, but together they took the first tunnel and followed its uneven path with shadows fluttering eerily around them, until

Ellen's nerve threatened to break altogether and she refused to go any further.

They turned back, stumbling in the near darkness, until they returned to the chamber. From here, Meg led her young companion back into the tunnel from which they had first entered. The shaft entrance was a distant square of daylight far, far above. Meg held the candle high and tried to estimate the distance from the tunnel floor to the first of the rungs in the wall. Seven feet? Eight?

Even if she could somehow boost Ellen up onto her shoulders, the little girl still wouldn't be able to reach the first rung.

Around them, the mine groaned and it seemed to Meg that the earth shifted restlessly overhead.

We have to get out of here . . .

An idea suddenly occurred to her, and she said, 'Come with me.'

Together the girls returned to the chamber and Meg passed the candle to

Ellen and then began to examine all the boxes and tea chests with which the place was filled. Many were empty, the remainder filled with odds and ends of junk that would offer no solution.

But the boxes themselves . . .

'We're going to build ourselves a staircase,' Meg decided. 'Something that will help us reach that first rung.'

Energised by the idea, she set to work with a will, dragging empty tea chests from the chamber out into the tunnel, where she turned them upside-down and then tried to arrange them into some sort of pyramid shape. It took six chests in all, three at the base, two at the second level and one at the third.

By the time she was finished she was a bedraggled mess, and the candle was little more than a guttering, half-inch stub that threatened to go out at any second.

As Meg sleeved her forehead she looked up at the distant square of sky and was surprised to see how much time had gone by. Already it must be late afternoon and scudding clouds had darkened the sky noticeably.

With no time to lose now, she lifted Ellen onto the first chest and held her hand as the child climbed up onto the second. The makeshift structure shifted a little, but held firm.

'Be careful, now . . . '

Ellen raised herself up onto the third chest and reached for one of the rungs in the wall. When her small fingers closed around it, Meg heaved a sigh of relief.

Then the candle flickered and went out.

Darkness claimed the mine.

' . . . M-Meg . . . ?'

'I'm here, Ellen. Just start climbing and take your time.'

'All . . . all right . . . '

Working by feel, Meg slowly and carefully scaled her makeshift staircase and then felt around until her hands finally closed on one of the rungs. She carefully began to climb.

Ahead of her, Ellen was making good

progress, her silhouette plain to see against the lowering sky.

A few moments later it began to rain, and the rungs grew slippery. 'Be careful now,' Meg called, her eyelids flickering as the drizzle peppered her upturned face. 'Just take your time and make sure you hang on tight.'

'I . . . I will,' Ellen called back.

On they climbed, with breeze-blown clouds racing each other across the dark sky above them. Meg could hear the wind now, as it whistled through the rusty waterwheel and slipped around the fallen remains of the mine buildings.

And then, at last, Ellen vanished over the lip of the entrance, returning a moment later to call down, 'I'm at the top!'

Meg sagged a little, for the child's safety had been her greatest concern. She continued to climb until she felt Ellen's hands on her arms, the little girl doing her best to help Meg out of the shaft.

Meg stumbled from the shaft and staggered to her feet. They'd made it — they were free!

But there was no time to waste. They had to make their way back to Penderow and report what had happened.

And that was when a voice behind them snapped harshly, 'Stay right where you are!'

19

Ennor rapped sharply at Constable Hendy's front door and then stood back so that he could keep a wary eye on his prisoner. Beside him, his hands tied tight behind his back, the man he and Jack had christened One-Eye glared at him.

'I won't talk, you know,' the man said in a low, sullen rasp. 'The only reason I told your friend as much as I did was because he had a pistol pointed at me.'

'Well, you'd do well to remember that *I'm* holding the pistol now,' Ennor returned, brandishing the weapon Jack had given him. 'And after what you and your friends have done to my daughter and Jack's, you should be grateful I haven't already used it on you!'

The front door opened and Constable Hendy looked from one of his callers to the other.

'Ennor Deveral!' he breathed. 'What the deuce is goin' on?'

Ennor said, 'This man here — '

'I mean about your daughter, man!' interrupted the policeman.

Ennor eyed him sharply, suddenly fearful as to what he might hear next. 'What about her?' he demanded.

'Mrs Gwynn from Tredray Lane called in earlier this afternoon to say she'd seen your daughter and Masterman's little girl nosing around Ned Magowan's old place. Then she said Abel Keskey and Yestin Treffale turned up and they all went away in Abel's wagon.'

'When was this?' snapped Ennor.

'This mornin'.'

'And what have you done about it?'

'I've had my hands full with this Masterman business, and since I didn't see as any crime had been committed, I just thought — '

'That's your trouble, Tom,' said Ennor, 'you *don't* think!'

'Now, see here — '

'No, *you* see here,' Ennor grated.

237

'Abel Keskey and Yestin Treffale are in this wrecking business up to their necks, and so are the brothers.'

Hendy's face slackened. 'The *Banes*? No, you're — '

'I've a witness here who'll confirm it,' said Ennor, and glancing at One-Eye he added meaningfully, '*if* he wants to escape the hangman's rope.'

★ ★ ★

As far as Ennor was concerned, it took far too long to explain everything for Constable Hendy's benefit, but the policeman wouldn't be rushed. First of all he listened to everything Ennor told him about Jack's plan to force the wreckers into action and his hope of catching them red-handed. Then Ennor explained One-Eye's part in the plan and how, upon questioning, he had reluctantly implicated Abel Keskey and the Banes.

Hendy had then turned to the surly prisoner and questioned him at some length to confirm Ennor's version of events. At first One-Eye had refused to talk, until Ennor reminded him that he would hang for sure unless he turned King's Evidence. Then it became difficult to shut him up.

'Where's Jack Masterman now?' asked Hendy when One-Eye finally fell silent.

'He found the horse this here cove used to ride out to the Point and then went on to Wheal Hazel to rescue the girls.'

'He's still wanted for murder, you know.'

'Murder be damned!' Ennor exploded. 'Now, I've told you as much as I know about this business, so now I've a question for *you*, Tom Hendy! What do you propose to *do* about it?'

Hendy considered the matter for what, to Ennor, seemed like an eternity. 'I'll send a message to the garrison at Ludbury,' he decided. 'We'll draft in some soldiers.'

'And how long do you suppose that'll take?'

'I can't go up to Bane House on my own,' objected Hendy. 'Not if they're as dangerous as you claim.'

'Well, you can't afford to wait, either. Jack Masterman set a trap to catch these fellows, and they went for the bait. It's now or never, Tom.'

Hendy looked so completely out of his depth that Ennor almost felt sorry for him. *Almost.* But there was no time for sympathy just now; there was too much at stake.

'You want an army with you when you arrest those scallywags,' said Ennor, struck by a sudden inspiration. 'All right — I'll *give* you an army.'

'What do you mean?' asked Hendy.

'You've an army of men down there right now, in the harbour,' said Ennor. '*Fishermen*, Tom. Men of the sea, who know all too well just how cruel that sea can be for the unwary. Men who hate wreckers like the Banes with a passion.'

'But I can't just — !'

'Maybe you can't,' said Ennor, starting toward the front door. 'But I *can.* I'm going down there now and I'm going to round up as many good men as I can . . . and then we're going to march on Bane House.'

'You can't take the law into your own hands!'

'Then lead us,' said Ennor. 'And keep it legal!'

Hendy hesitated. He was old before his time and too fat to be really effective, but . . . but these were his people, this was his stretch of coast, and there could be no doubt now as to the brothers' guilt.

'Let me lock this miserable rascal up,' he said. 'And then we'll be on our way.'

★ ★ ★

Out at Wheal Hazel, Meg and Ellen turned just as Abel Keskey came out of the tumbledown building he'd taken shelter in and starting running toward them. Spotting his wagon nearby, Meg realised that he must have stayed behind to keep an eye on them and make sure they didn't escape.

Instinctively she stepped in front of Ellen, to shield her from the growing threat of violence.

'I don't know how you got out of there,' Keskey yelled, stabbing one finger toward the shaft, 'but get back down there right now!'

Without taking her eyes off the advancing man Meg said to Ellen, 'Run!'

'But — '

'*Just run!*'

Ellen turned and bolted across the grass as fast as she could go. Keskey stared after her, torn between pursuing her and dealing with Meg. Perceiving Meg to be the greater threat, he continued toward her, his pace seemingly unstoppable.

'You'll get back down that shaft even if I have to throw you down there!' he promised, and before she could evade him he had her by the arms and was dragging her back toward the mine-entrance.

She fought him every step of the way, doing the best she could to dig her heels in and make herself a dead weight.

Keskey glared at her, his face straining with effort as he struggled to drag her along. His eyes were wide with fury; as he wheezed, she could smell sour beer-fumes on his breath.

Then, catching her by surprise, he suddenly pulled her to him so that she was caught in some sort of bear-hug, and while she was trapped thus he lifted her off her feet and more or less carried her closer to the mine entrance.

She wriggled like an eel to escape his awful embrace, but he was too strong and there was no resisting him.

Until —

All at once he stopped dead in his tracks, his eyes widened still further and he roared in pain.

He let go of Meg and Meg fell away from him. Then he whirled around until he could confront —

Ellen!

The little girl had come back for her. Now she faced this angry adult with as much courage as she could muster, and as he advanced upon her she kicked him for a second time, this time right in the shin.

As Keskey howled and swore, Meg almost threw herself onto his back to keep him from grabbing Ellen.

Keskey roared again, spun around to dislodge her, and her hold on him loosened, she fell and rolled several feet.

She heard Keskey scream and her head snapped around just in time to see the innkeeper teetering on the edge of the shaft, his arms making desperate wind-milling motions so that he might regain his balance. But it was no use — he was already too far gone, and even as she watched he screamed again and tipped backwards down the shaft.

A shockingly short time later there came a loud crash, and Keskey's scream ended abruptly.

For several seconds Meg and Ellen

just stared at each other, breathing hard and trembling in shock. Then Ellen ran across to Meg and straight into her arms. Meg held her close and thanked her for coming back, even though she really should have just kept going.

As she got back to her feet she wondered if the fall had killed the innkeeper, and whether or not she should hold herself responsible for his unhappy end. But in the next moment a voice came up to them from the bottom of the shaft.

'H . . . help . . .'

Meg felt a surge of relief. The fall hadn't killed Keskey, then.

'I think . . . I think I've . . . b-broken my leg!' the innkeeper called up from the darkness.

Meg licked her lips. 'We'll . . . we'll fetch help!' she called back.

'Not that you deserve it!' added Ellen.

Together the girls started across to the wagon, until a new sound caught their attention — the sound of a horse's hooves, coming ever closer at speed.

Meg thought desperately, *No, no, they can't catch us again* . . .

A second later the rider appeared around the corner of what had once been a storage shed, leaning low across the glistening neck of his galloping horse, his black hair flying wildly around his head.

'It's Dad!' squealed Ellen.

Meg's eyelids fluttered. *Jack!* She had no idea what he was doing here, only that just the sight of him made her believe that everything would turn out right after all.

Changing course, they both ran to meet him, and when he was near enough he virtually threw himself down off the horse while it was still moving, and ran to gather them both in his arms.

'Are you all right?' he asked urgently. And again, 'Are you both all right?'

'Yes, Dad.'

He was so relieved he hugged Ellen close and kissed the top of her head, then turned to Meg and —

He hesitated for only the briefest moment; then, wordlessly, he pulled her close and kissed her fully on the lips.

It was a long, heartfelt kiss that carried with it all the pent-up passion in them both, and though Meg never wanted it to end, she knew they had other more pressing concerns just then.

'What's happening, Jack?' she asked breathlessly when they finally broke apart.

'It's a long story,' Jack replied, and reaching into his jacket he produced Polly and passed the doll to a delighted Ellen.

He told Meg everything as quickly as he could, then. 'When I left Ennor, he was taking this one-eyed man down to Constable Hendy. Our hope now is that Hendy will take action to clean out that rats' nest once and for all.'

Tears moved in Meg's eyes. 'Then you've done it,' she husked. 'You've proved my Da' innocent.'

He nodded. 'I think so, Meg. I think we have.'

'But Hendy still thinks you're guilty of . . . '

Jack's face was grim in the drizzle. 'Let's just deal with one problem at a time,' he said. 'Now come on, you two. Let me tie my horse to the back of Keskey's wagon and then we'll go back to Penderow and summon the doctor for that poor wretch down the shaft.'

20

As dusk began to steal across the sky, the stables behind Bane House became a riot of activity. Yestin Treffale strode back and forth, snapping orders like a regimental sergeant-major, his army the rough-and-ready drifters and vagabonds Abel Keskey had recruited for tonight's crooked enterprise. As they prepared the two wagons for travel and considered the looting of the *McNair*, there was tension and greed in the air.

But —

'I don't like it,' muttered Cador, pacing the sitting room floor like a caged tiger. 'I mean, what happened to Bennets?'

Talan made no reply, but he too was concerned. They had sent the one-eyed man known as Robert Bennets to the Point to deliver their message to Ennor Deveral. Once that was done he should have returned to Bane House. But he hadn't. Talan didn't like to think what that might signify.

'If something went wrong,' said Cador, 'we'd do well to forget tonight's little enterprise.'

Talan looked at him in surprise. 'Forget the chance to make ourselves a small fortune?' he countered. 'We might never get our hands on such a cargo again!'

'Maybe not,' Cador scowled, 'but that's a chance I'd be prepared to take.'

'You, the one who was so sick of having to watch every penny?'

'I've got a bad feeling about this,' Cador replied restlessly. 'Too many things have happened . . . the Masterman woman — '

Talan's expression tightened at the mention of Elizabeth. In the short time they had been together he had developed feelings for her he had not foreseen and which still grieved him. 'We solved that problem,' he snapped.

'Did we?' Cador ran the back of one

hand across his mouth. He wanted a drink very badly indeed. 'Or in framing Masterman for his wife's murder did we just force that girl, Deveral's daughter, to think again about what happened to Ned Magowan and come close to revealing the whole sorry business?'

'That's ridiculous!'

'Then why did she go back to Ned's cottage? What made her look around until she found his confession — a confession *we*, dear brother, never even *suspected*, but which could have put a noose around each of our necks?'

'What good did it do her?' argued Talan.

Cador made no reply, but he couldn't suppress a shiver. It was only by chance that Treffale's instincts had told him to keep an eye on Meg. If not for that —

'You know, of course, that she and the child will have to die,' he said.

Talan nodded. 'Of course. They can identify Yestin and Keskey — '

' — who in turn could identify *us*.'

'Yes, yes, I know all that.'

'And now Bennets.'

Impulsively Cador suddenly heeled around. 'Let us abandon tonight's enterprise,' he said, and Talan saw with some surprise that his brother was genuinely fearful. He had never seen fear in him before, and it unsettled him to see it now.

'No,' he said. 'We see it through, and come tomorrow's dawn we'll be set up for a good long while.'

Cador went over to the window and stared out beyond the network of wooden scaffolding. 'Tomorrow . . . ' he said, and it made it seem very far away.

Before they could continue the conversation the doors flew open and Treffale came hurrying in. 'Trouble,' he said.

'What is it?' asked Talan.

'I don't know how and I don't know why, but . . . '

'Go on,' said Talan, his voice low.

'I think the game's up for us,' said Treffale.

Talan and Cador followed him to the front door and Treffale swung it wide. In the gathering dusk they saw a twenty-strong group of local men marching down the gravel drive toward the house, with Constable Hendy and Ennor Deveral at their head.

Talan swore under his breath. He wanted to believe that there was some other reason for their presence, but knew there could only be one. Had Bennets talked? Or Keskey? Had the Deveral girl somehow escaped from the mine and raised the alarm?

'What are we going to do?' Cador asked tightly.

Before Talan could reply, the mob, spotting them, came to a halt about thirty yards from the front of the house and Constable Hendy called, 'My lords, I'd appreciate it if you would come quietly!'

From the corner of his eye Talan saw Cador sway a little and grimaced. His brother was going to be of little use in whatever came next. Stepping forward,

Talan called, 'How dare you use that tone with me! What is the meaning of this assembly?'

Ennor shoved past Hendy. 'It's all up, Bane! Hendy's here to arrest you for deliberately wrecking the *Persephone* and others, and we're here to support him!'

The men Keskey had gathered for tonight's business had wandered cautiously around to the front of the house to see what all the shouting was about. Now, sensing that the game, as Ennor had so rightly said, was up, they began muttering darkly among themselves — and then made a run for it.

'*Get them!*' yelled Hendy, and the sea-toughened fishermen behind him moved quickly to do just that. In seconds a series of scuffles and struggles had broken out, but by that time Talan had already seen enough.

He turned and pushed past Treffale. 'We've got to get away,' he said.

Treffale grabbed him by the sleeve and pulled him around. 'And how do you propose we do that?'

His temper snapping, Talan snarled, 'Take your hand off me!' and without warning he lashed out.

Pain exploded in Treffale's jaw and he staggered a step with the force of the blow. 'You — !'

But Talan and Cador were already retreating back through the house, intent on escape.

Treffale looked around. Ennor Deveral was hurrying toward him, with Hendy lumbering along behind. He was seized by panic, by the thought of the hangman tucking the noose up tight beneath his left ear.

On impulse he stepped out to meet them, dragging Ned Magowan's confession from his pocket and holding it out. 'You're right!' he cried. 'The Banes are behind it all, even the murder of the Masterman woman! I had no choice but to go along with them — '

Hearing Treffale's desperate attempt to plead his innocence at their expense, Cador suddenly spun back and tore one of a matched pair of flintlocks from where he had secreted it at his waistband.

He drew back the hammer and pulled the trigger. There was a loud boom, a sudden cloud of smoke, and Treffale made a strange gurgling sound deep in his throat, then fell forward onto his face with a fatal bullet-wound in his back.

Constable Hendy hauled to a stop, his mouth dropping open in shock, but Ennor reacted differently, yelling, '*Get them, lads! Sharpish now, before they get away!*'

The brothers crossed the dismal lobby at a desperate run, their footsteps clattering through the empty house. Cador followed Talan through the darkened kitchen, knocking pots and pans everywhere in their haste, until they came to the back door. Then they burst out into the coming night, both breathing hard, each as scared as the other.

'What do we do?' pleaded Cador.

'Where shall we go?'

'There!' said Talan, sprinting toward one of the two wagons with which they had been hoping to transport their booty later tonight.

He scrambled for the seat with Cador at his heels, then tore the reins from where they had been wrapped around the brake-handle and slapped them hard against the rumps of the team-animals.

The wagon immediately lurched into movement.

Up ahead, the fishermen came racing around the corner of the house, intent on stopping them. Up on the wagon both brothers heard them shouting to each other, and then the fishermen headed for the nearby scaffolding and started to shake the structure as hard as they could.

Slowly it lurched away from the house and began to tip over.

'*Nooo!*' cried Cador.

The wagon rattled on, Talan unable to stop it now even had he wanted to.

Beside him, Cador's blue eyes went round as he watched with awful fascination as the scaffolding slowly, slowly keeled over, promising to crush them —

Then the wagon was turning the corner and gravel was spitting up beneath its spinning wheels, and the scaffolding was collapsing with a sound like thunder behind them.

'We . . . we made it!'

Cador's tone said he could hardly believe it.

Talan was too busy controlling the horses to reply. Under his guidance the wagon rocked and swayed along the drive toward the lane beyond . . . and all Ennor, Hendy and the fishermen could do was watch as the Banes made good their escape.

21

Jack was driving Abel Keskey's wagon back toward Penderow with Meg and Ellen at his side when, up ahead, another wagon suddenly pitched out onto the lane ahead of them and turned left. Having already caught the sound of raised voices, what sounded very much like a pistol-shot and then a terrifying clatter on the damp early-evening air, Jack immediately tensed, fearing more trouble.

'Who was in that wagon?' he demanded.

Meg strained her eyes to see through the misty drizzle. Finally she breathed, 'The Banes!'

'The brothers behind all this trouble?'

'Yes.'

'Then something's gone wrong with the plan to arrest them,' he decided, and quickly thrust the reins into Meg's hands.

'What are you doing?' she asked, startled.

'I'm going to make sure they don't get away!' he replied, and leapt down off the moving wagon.

As it passed him he reached up, deftly untied his borrowed horse from the tailgate and swung astride in one athletic movement. A moment later he splashed past them at a canter, going in pursuit of the fleeing brothers.

Meanwhile, beside Talan on the swaying wagon seat, Cador looked back over one shoulder to satisfy himself that they really had left Hendy and the others behind. Instead he gasped.

'What is it?' asked Talan, not taking his eyes off the lane in front of them.

'A horseman,' said Cador, dragging his second flintlock from his waistband. 'I don't know him, but from his looks I think he might be the lighthouse-keeper.'

'*Masterman?* I thought he was supposed to be on the run.'

'Aye, me too. But there he is, large as

life — and he's gaining on us, brother!'

Talan's profile hardened. 'Fix him,' he said.

Cador needed no second urging. Awkwardly he climbed over the back of the seat and staggered along the wagon-bed toward the tailgate. The rider was no more than thirty feet behind them now, and gaining fast.

Jaw muscles bunching, Cador carefully brought his pistol up to line on their pursuer . . . and fired.

He smiled cruelly as Jack Masterman grunted and pitched forward across his horse's neck.

* * *

Meg hauled back on the reins to bring the wagon to a halt just as her father, Constable Hendy and their hastily-convened army appeared at the head of the gravel drive, the fishermen shoving their prisoners roughly ahead of them.

Ennor hurried over to the wagon. '*Douter!*' he cried. 'Little princess!'

Relief at seeing them both safe and well choked him then, and it was a moment before he could speak again.

'Where's Jack?'

'He's gone after the Banes,' said Meg.

A mutter of approval ran through the fishermen.

'But he'll not go after them alone,' Ennor decided. 'Shift over, *douter*. He might need help when he catches up with them!'

'I'm comin', too!' said Hendy. 'Got to keep this all legal!'

'Well get a move on then!'

A moment later the horses leaned forward into their traces and the wagon set off after Jack and the men whose escape he was so determined to foil.

★ ★ ★

The bullet slammed into Jack's left arm and he slumped loosely over his galloping horse. He had never known pain like the all-consuming, white-hot

262

pain that knifed through him in that moment, and it was all he could do to keep from passing out.

Somehow he thrust himself back up, his left arm now hanging uselessly at his side, the world spinning drunkenly around him — and when Cador saw him recover and jab his heels into his horse's flanks to urge it to even greater speed, he panicked.

'He's still coming!' he yelled to Talan. 'I shot him and yet he's still coming!'

Up ahead and to his right Talan saw the proud spire of the Penderow Point lighthouse racing ever closer. If they could just outrace their pursuer and make it through the village, they might yet manage to escape capture. But that was beginning to sound increasingly unlikely — unless they stopped Jack Masterman for good.

Talan slapped the horses unmercifully, and they responded by hauling the rocking, jolting wagon ever faster along the rutted lane. As they sped past the unmanned lighthouse Talan turned at the waist, fixed his brother with a glare and yelled, 'Then reload your pistol, brother! Shoot him again, and keep on shooting him until he falls!'

Cador opened his mouth to respond — and then froze as something seemed to tear and splinter beneath them.

Talan said, 'Wha — ?'

He realised that Cador was no longer looking at him, but rather at something *beyond* him.

He twisted back to face front again . . . and saw that it was already too late to escape his fate.

As the terrified horses swerved to the left so that they could follow the lane as it turned toward the village, the tongue of the wagon had ripped away from the running gear beneath the seat. The horses, suddenly free, continued on their way with manes flying. The wagon, however, stayed on its original course, speeding directly toward the edge of the cliff.

Jack was just in time to see the wagon and its two passengers fly out into thin air and then fall, fall, fall . . . only to finally crash against the merciless Devil's Teeth far, far below.

Then he finally gave in to the overwhelming pain and fell slackly from the saddle.

★   ★   ★

When Meg, Ennor and Ellen arrived in the wagon a few minutes later, they found the horse standing head-down beside Jack's still, rain-soaked body. As Meg threw herself down from the seat and splashed across to him, a low moan escaped her.

No . . . no . . . no . . .

She dropped to her knees beside him. He looked so pale, so lifeless —

Ennor and Ellen joined her. Ennor said, 'Is he — ?'

'He's still alive, Da,' said Meg, checking for his heartbeat, 'but I don't know for how long . . .'

Ellen dropped down beside him, cradled his head and started sobbing.

The sight broke Ennor's heart, but he gently pulled the child aside and then picked Jack up in his arms as if he were weightless.

He carried him into the cottage and set him down as gently as possible on his bed. Then he turned and left them to go and fetch Dr Trewin.

Meg held one of Jack's hands, Ellen the other. He lay still and oblivious to their presence. A short time later there was a soft knock at the door and Constable Hendy let himself inside.

'Is everything all right, miss?' he asked when Meg appeared at the bedroom door.

Not trusting herself to speak, Meg could only shrug.

'I owe you that apology,' the policeman said softly. 'And I give it sincerely from the bottom of my heart, as I will to your father, the next time I see him.' He swallowed as his eyes moved past her to the bedroom. 'I also owe that man in there an apology, too. He never killed his wife. Thanks to Yestin Treffale

I know that now. And thanks to Ned Magowan's confession, I know a lot more besides.'

'Thank you,' Meg said vaguely.

'*Meg!*'

Meg turned, jolted by the urgency in Ellen's tone. She hurried back to the bed, where Jack was looking up at her through pain-glazed eyes.

'Jack! We thought we'd lost you!' she said, taking his hand again.

'Not . . . yet . . . ' he managed. He reached out and stroked his daughter's hair. 'I love you, Ellen,' he croaked. And then, 'I love you too, Meg.'

Before she could reply his eyelids flicked and his head rolled to one side against the pillow.

'Jack!' Meg sobbed. 'Don't die. *Please* don't die . . . '

She felt hands on her shoulders then. It was Ennor, easing her away from the bed.

And then Dr Trewin was there, his coat wet from the rain, his black bag in hand. 'Go and wash your hands, Meg,' he said, studying his patient critically. 'I'm going to need help here.'

Meg blinked, sleeved her damp cheeks, nodded and went to do as he said. Ennor, meanwhile, took Ellen gently by the hand and led her from the room.

If ever there was a time for prayer, he thought, this was it.

★ ★ ★

A long time passed before the bedroom door opened again and Dr Trewin came outside. He looked down at Ellen and said, 'I think your father would like to see you now, young lady. You too, Ennor.' They hurried into the bedroom to find Jack, stripped to the waist, his wound now tended and bandaged, resting against his plumped-up pillows. Although still drowsy from the anaesthetic, he managed a weak smile for his visitors as Meg finished tucking him in with a clean coverlet.

'*Dad!*'

Ellen almost threw herself at him, but

remembered herself just in time and reached over to peck him gently on one cheek instead.

'Dad, are you going to be all right?' she asked.

He nodded. 'I was *always* going to be all right,' he replied weakly. 'So long as I knew you and Meg would be here when I woke up again.'

Ennor cleared his throat. 'Well,' he said, 'that's the thing about the light at Penderow. No matter what life throws at it, it always keeps the darkness at bay.'

Dr Trewin smiled indulgently. 'Jack here — or maybe I should call him your future son-in-law, Ennor? — he'll be fine, eventually. But in the meantime he'll need care — a lot of it.'

'He'll get it, too,' Meg said, and she squeezed Jack's hand.

'And this lighthouse will have need of a good man until he's ready to take up his duties again,' the doctor reminded them.

Ennor shrugged. 'Oh, I reckon I can manage that.'

269

'Then I'll be on my way,' said the doctor. 'Apparently I've got another patient waiting for me out at Wheal Hazel — Abel Keskey with a broken leg.'

He went as far as the door, then turned back. 'Why don't you go and make everyone a nice cup of tea, Ennor Deveral?' he said. 'I think these two lovebirds need some time to themselves, don't you?'

'Indeed I do,' said Ennor. And to Meg he said with mock severity, 'Look after that man, *douter*. Now that it appears I've got my good name back, he'll have a lot to live up to when he takes this place over again.'

'Oh, I will,' Meg replied. 'And looking after him starts right this minute.'

THE END

We do hope that you have enjoyed reading this large print book.

Did you know that all of our titles are available for purchase?

We publish a wide range of high quality large print books including:
Romances, Mysteries, Classics
General Fiction
Non Fiction and Westerns

Special interest titles available in large print are:
The Little Oxford Dictionary
Music Book, Song Book
Hymn Book, Service Book

Also available from us courtesy of Oxford University Press:
Young Readers' Dictionary
(large print edition)
Young Readers' Thesaurus
(large print edition)

For further information or a free brochure, please contact us at:
Ulverscroft Large Print Books Ltd.,
The Green, Bradgate Road, Anstey,
Leicester, LE7 7FU, England.
Tel: (00 44) **0116 236 4325**
Fax: (00 44) **0116 234 0205**

SOME EIGHTEEN SUMMERS

Lillie Holland

After eighteen years living a sheltered life as a vicar's daughter in Norfolk, Debbie Meredith takes work as a companion to the wealthy Mrs Caroline Dewbrey in Yorkshire. Travelling by train, she meets the handsome and charming Hugh Stacey. However, before long, Debbie is wondering why Mrs Dewbrey lavishes so much attention on her. And what of her son Alec's stance against her involvement with Hugh? Debbie then finds that she's just a pawn embroiled in a tragic vendetta . . .